She was run

Kiki backed up to the door and opened it, her hand twisting the knob around without her looking. She kept a close eye on Lacey, preparing herself for any crazy move she might make. She gave Lacey a weak wave.

"See you," Lacey said, a forced smile on her face.

Kiki closed the door behind her and hurried down the stairs and out of the house. She was certain now. The shoes were the final proof. Kiki felt a painful sadness knowing that Lacey could actually have committed murder.

Then her sadness turned to fear. Hope was right. But were they in over their heads? Kiki raced through the darkness toward the gate of the Pinkerton estate. She was running for her life.

Find out **Who Killed Peggy Sue?**
Read:

Available from Teens · Mandarin

Who Killed Peggy Sue?

Jailbird

Created by Eileen Goudge

Teens · Mandarin

First published in the USA 1991
by Viking Penguin, a division of Penguin Books USA Inc.
First published in Great Britain 1992
by Teens · Mandarin
an imprint of Mandarin Paperbacks
Michelin House, 81 Fulham Road, London SW3 6RB
Reprinted 1992

Mandarin is an imprint of the Octopus Publishing Group,
a division of Reed International Books Ltd

ISBN 0 7497 1076 4

A CIP catalogue record for this title
is available from the British Library

Printed in Great Britain
by Cox & Wyman Ltd, Reading, Berkshire

Jailbird

CHAPTER 1

"Lacey! Lacey! Lacey!" chanted the boisterous cheering section on the left side of the auditorium. Lacey Pinkerton sat onstage, looking down on her sea of admirers. She waved her hand in the air and smiled. A gracious Queen. I'm going to win. I'm gonna be the Peach Blossom Queen. Just call me Pretty Peggy Sue.

Raven Cruz and Kiki De Santis flanked her on either side. The competition. Lacey tried to block them out as she basked in all the attention. No way was Lacey going to let Kiki, Miss Sugar and Spice, ex–best friend and current biggest enemy, ruin all the excitement. Her fans probably numbered all of one— Bobby Deeter. The drip was so smitten by Kiki that he actually thought his girlfriend stood a chance of winning. He was sitting in the front row, holding a bouquet of red roses in his hand, staring dreamily at Kiki.

1

Forget it, Bobby. Kiki is just a few seconds away from becoming a forgotten name in the Paradiso record book. Second-place, Kiki De Santis, Lacey thought. If she's lucky.

Lacey gave Kiki the slight edge over Raven. Even though Raven was Lacey's arch-enemy, she had to admit the girl had style. She didn't have money, but somehow she managed to look like a million bucks. She was smart too, which is why Lacey couldn't figure out why she'd ruined her chance at winning the crown. Ever since Raven had quit SCAM—Students Concerned About the Mall—the do-good organization that she had founded, her popularity had gone way downhill. Raven and her grass-roots movement had very nearly succeeded in destroying Lacey and Vaughn Cutter's fathers' plan to build a mall in the scrublands, the largest piece of undeveloped property in Paradiso. But out of the blue Raven had come into school one day last week and quit. No explanation. SCAM was dead and so were Raven's chances of winning Peggy Sue. Lacey could taste the victory.

The cheering escalated. Penny Bolton and Renée Henderson, Lacey's loyal followers who called themselves the Pinks, were screaming their heads off. Real pep-squad leaders.

Lacey flashed her best Hollywood smile to the crowd. Hollywood was where she was headed, too, with the screen test that went along with winning the

Peach Blossom crown. Lacey soaked up the glory—
this was where she belonged.

It was clear that everyone's spirits were riding high
on the recent news that April Lovewell's murderer
had been caught and was now in jail. April had been
Peach Blossom Queen less than a day when her stiff,
cold body was found stuffed in her cousin Hope Hubbard's locker, a big gash in her head and a nylon rope
tied tightly around her neck. Idyllic Paradiso was immediately plunged into a horrible, inescapable nightmare.

Lacey, however, had reasons to be depressed other
than April's murder. First there was her breakup with
Jess Gardner. And the one with Vaughn. Far worse
was the ongoing mess with her father. The welts on
Lacey's legs, and her black eye, were the result of
Calvin's most recent drunken outbursts.

But now, with Spike Navarrone's arrest, Lacey's
biggest problem had been put to rest. It was ridicu-
lous, of course; she could see that now, but until yesterday she'd actually convinced herself that one of
her parents was a murderer. How far would Daddy
go, she wondered, to make Paradiso look like an un-
safe place that *needed* a mall to keep kids off the
streets? And what about Mother? To Darla Pinkerton
—the former Peach Blossom Queen—it was unthink-
able to have a loser for a daughter. The only person
more furious than Lacey that April had won the contest was Darla.

Of course it was all nonsense. Mother and Daddy might lose their tempers at times, but they wouldn't do something as tacky as murder. Lacey had allowed herself to be misled by common, foolish public opinion. Willa Flicker's condemning articles in the Paradiso *Record* had fueled the fire. And then there had been T. J. the D. J., blasting Daddy on Daddy's own radio station.

But Spike ("Carlos," as the newspaper called him) had been captured and had confessed to the murder of April, his girlfriend who was pregnant with his never-to-be-born baby. Hope Hubbard and Jess Gardner had found the murder weapon, a big monkey wrench, under a ponderosa pine near school. And they'd found Spike's and April's initials carved into the tree—A. L. + S. N., it said, with a big heart around the whole thing.

Now Spike was in jail, and the horrible tragedy and all the mistrust and false accusations were finally over. The dark shadow that had hung so heavily over Lacey and her family was lifted. Today marked the beginning of a new dawn in Paradiso. Lacey would be named Queen, and the California sunshine would feel brighter than ever.

"Can you hear me, dudes?" Dwight Appleby, principal and first-class dweeb, tapped at the microphone and waved his free hand in the air, trying to quiet the crowd. The sweat stains that marked the armpits of his pea green leisure suit could be seen from the last

4

row of bleachers in the auditorium. "Please, kids. Shhh . . ." Quieting the masses was no small task. It was impossible to get their attention. "And the winner of the Peach Blossom contest is . . ." Total silence was achieved.

"The winner of the Peach Blossom contest, Pretty Peggy Sue, is sitting right here on this stage," he said, leaving everybody hanging.

Come on. Make the announcement, you dweeb. Lacey closed her eyes, picturing herself wearing a crown and looking down on the entire town of Paradiso kneeling humbly before their royal Queen.

"Now, now. Please. Bear with me," Appleby pleaded. "Before I announce the winner, I have a few things I'd like to say."

"Just say Lacey!" a voice boomed from the left side of the auditorium. A big cheer went up from the section where Lacey's friends were, and she stood and waved.

"No. Say Kiki!" Bobby Deeter, front and center, stood up alone, pumping a lame fist in the air. A weak "Let's go, Kiki" was drowned out by the Lacey section's shout of "Sit down!"

In the back of the audience three members of the now-defunct SCAM waved banners that spelled out RAVEN, WE STILL BELIEVE IN YOU—AND IN THE SCRUBLANDS.

Lacey gave a little elbow to Kiki. "Democracy rules, Kiki. I always said you should have conceded," she whispered. "Neither of you little do-gooders stands a chance."

"We'll see," Kiki said, shooting Lacey a glare.

"Okay, okay." Appleby hemmed and hawed. He scratched at the top of his round, practically bald head. It was clear that he wasn't going to get any sympathy from the crowd until he announced the winner. He read from a prepared speech. "The Peach Blossom Festival is just eleven days away. I can't wait. And I bet you can't either." Could he be any duller? "Now I'm sure you'd all like to know who our Queen will be."

"Tell us before we graduate and go to college," Eddie Hagenspitzel, class clown and former Lacey groupie, yelled.

"*If* you graduate," Appleby warned. The crowd cracked up. Every once in a while the Dweeb managed to get even. "Like I said," he continued, "I'm sure you are all dying to know who it's going to be." He opened his arms, motioning toward Lacey. "Lacey Pinkerton?" A huge roar from the audience filled the auditorium.

Definitely. He was just prolonging the wait.

"Or will it be Kiki De Santis?" Another pause as there was a long and loud applause for Kiki.

I can't believe she gets any cheers at all, Lacey thought.

"Or will it be Raven Cruz?" Appleby asked. A

warm round of applause for Raven sounded as the banners in the back waved again.

"The committee had a very difficult time deciding. Really, it could have gone to any of our three fine candidates." Appleby looked offstage and motioned to someone who was waiting in the wings to come join him. Then he signaled to the sound booth. "Music, please," he called out.

To the rocking tune of Buddy Holly's "Peggy Sue," Appleby welcomed his guest onstage. "Boys and girls, let's welcome your friend and mine, the one and only T. J. the D. J."

His hair slicked back, T. J. had donned a black-leather jacket, a bright white T-shirt, blue jeans, and shiny black wing tips in honor of the fifties theme of this year's Festival. Paradiso's all-time favorite deejay took the stage to a thunderous roar of excitement. "T. J., T. J., T. J." He carried the coveted Peach Blossom crown with him on a red velvet pillow with gold tassels.

"Whoa, hip cats and chicks. I love you all. Each and every one of you," T. J. said.

Except me, Lacey thought with a rush of nervousness. She remembered T. J.'s biting comments on KPOP about her family and their connection with April's murder. T. J. had gotten himself fired from the radio station that Lacey's father owned, but he had also helped rally a lot of people against the

Pinkertons. Now here he was, on stage, right next to Lacey.

"Friends, T. J.'s got some good news. And," he paused, "he's got some even *better* news. First, the good news. Believe it or not, your main man T. J. is coming home. That's right. KPOP loves me after all, baby. The big bossman has given ol' T. J. his job back. So you better tune in to KPOP, the world's greatest radio station."

That must mean T. J. and Daddy made up! Lacey thought. The whole town will love Daddy for being so forgiving and rehiring T. J. And now, T. J.'s going to present me with the crown. Today really is the best day ever!

T. J. reached into his back pocket and pulled out a sealed envelope. The moment had finally come. "And now for the great news. Yours truly, T. J. the D. J., am honored to announce this year's Peach Blossom winner. Let me just tear open this envelope . . . see what's inside . . . Well, well, indeed, this is a beautiful moment. Three beautiful contestants. And our third-place winner—Miss Raven Cruz. Let's give her a big cheer." Raven stood and smiled graciously.

As expected. And you're lucky to even be onstage with us. Okay, you're next, Kiki. Number two. Lacey shifted in her seat, patted her hair in place, and moistened her lips, getting ready for her best Miss America wave.

"And now for our second-place winner . . ."

8

Lacey looked at Kiki and grinned.

"Our lady-in-waiting, Miss Lacey Pinkerton! Come on, let's hear it, folks!"

Lacey froze. *What? A lady-in-waiting? Me? To her?*

"Everybody!" T. J. boomed, "I humbly but regally present to you, the good citizens of Paradiso High, our Peach Blossom Queen, KIKI—DE—SANTIS! Pretty Peggy Sue!"

Lacey was in total shock. Next to her, Kiki was rising to her feet. T. J. placed the rhinestone-studded crown on her head and gave her a huge, warm hug. Kiki turned pink. Then he knelt down before her.

"Your Highness," he said, reaching out his hand. Kiki took it and he gave it a little kiss. She waved to the crowd and performed a humble curtsy. The crowd's cheers were deafening.

Lacey slumped in her chair. Impossible. There has to be a mistake. But as she looked over at Kiki, she saw a winner's smile on her face. A Queen's smile, complete with a tear of happiness trickling down her cheek.

And Raven, who had also lost, was congratulating Kiki. Lacey swore she heard her say that Kiki had deserved to win. She doesn't mean a word of it, Lacey thought. It's all an act.

Lacey listened in misery to Principal Appleby's words of praise for Queen Kiki. So kind, so beautiful. So special. He commended her for her outstanding work establishing the April Lovewell Memorial Foundation. "Thanks to Kiki, and with the help of April's fine art teacher, Mr. Mark Woolery, the April Lovewell Memorial Foundation will benefit from the upcoming exhibition and auction of Miss Lovewell's beautiful artwork. I might add that I hope to see many of you at the exhibit this weekend. Again, none of this would have been possible without the unselfish dedication and concern on the part of one student. Kiki De Santis. Truly it was an act of genuine goodness."

Lacey wanted to plug her ears as the Dweeb rambled on about Kiki. She was sure that Kiki's "act of genuine goodness" was just that—an act. But it had helped win her the crown. And all the rumors about Lacey and her family and the murder had made Lacey lose. It just wasn't fair.

Lacey wished she could sink right into the floor and disappear. She wanted to be alone, without anybody bothering her for a long, long time. But as the assembly came to a close, her still-faithful fans, the Pinks, were waiting for her at the foot of the stage.

"Don't bum, Lacey. It's okay. You should have won," Renée said, putting a sympathetic hand on Lacey's shoulder. "At least you finished second. You'll still have a big role in the Festival celebration."

"Great. Playing second fiddle to Kiki. A big role, I'm sure. Gee, I can't wait," Lacey pouted.

"Hey, Lacey," Penny said. "There's still eleven

days. And you *are* runner-up. Anything could happen. You never know."

"Don't give me any ideas, Pen. I'm mad enough right now to take care of that little jerk once and for all."

"Really sorry, Lacey," a sympathetic Janice Campbell said.

Lacey was barely listening. She glanced over at Kiki again. Hope Hubbard and heartthrob Jess were fawning over her. Vaughn was there too. And Bobby Deeter, of course. And practically everyone in the world. It was pure horror.

"I'm out of here, guys," Lacey said, heading for the exit. "I've got more important things to do than drool over Kiki De Santis."

"Hey, Lace. Wait up!" Penny followed, her tennis shoes squeaking on the linoleum floor. "I'm here for you, you know. I always am." Perky little Penny Bolton was Lacey's strongest supporter. Her petite build and impish face could be so misleading. Penny was the biggest gossipmonger in school.

Lacey managed a smile. "I know you want to help, Pen. I love you for that. You too, Renée. But I gotta be alone for a while." She turned and ran outside. She couldn't hold back the tears a second longer. As soon as she was by herself, the flood began. Lacey ran to her car and slumped down in the driver's seat, burying her head in her hands. She had blown it again.

11

Mother will never speak to me, she thought, her body going tense. She didn't know what to do next. Penny and Renée would just sit around and mope with her. But she couldn't go home. Facing her parents at a time like this would be the worst. She revved up the Ferrari, screeched out of the parking lot, and started driving. It didn't matter where. The farther away, the better. Away from Paradiso, away from failure.

CHAPTER 2

Kiki drove down Old Town Road toward the center of town, remembering the only time she had been inside the Paradiso police station. Her fourth-grade class had been given the grand tour of the station. She remembered being fingerprinted by Sheriff Rodriguez that day. Just for fun, to see what it was like to be a criminal. Now she was on her way to visit one, an alleged murderer.

She stopped the Isuzu Trooper at a red light. As she waited, the few people at the intersection with her tooted their horns at her and waved.

"Congratulations, Kiki dear," Mrs. Purdy called out from her station wagon. "I mean, Pretty Peggy Sue."

"Way to go, Kiki," Mr. Gillman, Emily's father, cheered as he pulled up in the next lane. "You'll make a beautiful Queen."

Kiki waved back. "Thank you," she said, smiling.

The congratulations and good-luck wishes had been going nonstop since the announcement. She still couldn't get used to being called beautiful. With her shoulder-length brown hair, slightly crooked smile, and boyish figure, Kiki had always considered herself just average. It was really a special feeling to be admired by everyone around her; she could feel her self-confidence growing. Still, Kiki had an unsettled feeling inside her, a feeling that she might be reigning over a town that had falsely accused one of its citizens.

She had found Spike at April's grave yesterday afternoon. Spike had looked so terrified when the police sirens started wailing in the distance. He had started to run, and he could have easily gotten away. But Kiki had tested him. "If you run, you're admitting you're guilty. If you're innocent, stay," she had called after him. Kiki could see the fright racing through his body. Yet Spike had stopped dead still and had willingly let Sheriff Rodriguez take him in.

But instead of telling the sheriff he was innocent, Spike had confessed to killing April. Kiki was shocked. Why had he quit running in the cemetery? Why had he insisted to her that he hadn't done it? When she'd looked into his eyes yesterday, she'd believed him. Now she didn't know what to think.

She pulled the Trooper into the visitors' parking lot in front of the police station. Right smack in the middle of town for everyone to see. Kiki knew people would talk when they found out she was visiting Spike. But she didn't care. Even though her head told her to stay away, her heart insisted that she go to Spike. There was something mysterious about him that she couldn't resist. Kiki knew she was playing with fire, but she was drawn to Spike, and there was no turning back.

Sheriff Rodriguez was sitting behind his desk doing some paperwork when Kiki walked in. A broad smile spread across his tan face when he saw her. "Well, this is certainly a pleasure. Hello, Miss De Santis. May I congratulate the Queen?"

"Thank you, sir."

"You know, I was hoping I'd get the opportunity to see you before the rest of Paradiso took up all your time. I was going to call you at home to ask if you'd pose for a photo with me. Would you mind? It really would be great for public relations to have a picture of the Peach Blossom Queen with the sheriff, don't you think?"

Kiki shrugged. "Well, yeah. I guess." I wonder if he'd still want to pose with me if he knew why I came here? Sheriff Rodriguez sure wasn't going to make things easy for her.

"It'll just take a second to set up." As the sheriff got out the camera, Kiki looked around the office, wondering where Spike was being held. She had some recollection of the jail cell being in a dark, seedy corner of the basement. Or did that image come from

15

watching too many bad TV movies? Kiki didn't know. In fact, she wasn't even sure there was a basement. She saw a closed door on the far wall of the office that she figured must lead to the jail cell.

The sheriff got the camera ready—the same camera he used for mug shots. He chose the American flag as a background. "The good ol' red, white, and blue," he said as he set the timer.

Kiki felt a little strange saluting the flag and having the sheriff's arm wrapped proudly around her when she was really there to visit an accused murderer. But she smiled for the camera as best she could and was glad to make the sheriff so happy.

"Perfect. I'll frame it and we'll hang it for everyone to see." He pointed to the wall behind his desk. "Pardon me, Kiki. I didn't even ask you why you came here."

"That's okay, sir. I came because I'd like to visit Spike," she said boldly.

"Carlos Navarrone?" A look of surprise replaced the sheriff's smile. He picked up the papers from his desk. "I was in the middle of finishing up his forms now. Tragic," he said, shaking his head. "I really thought he was innocent. Even when I brought him in. But Carlos admitted his guilt, so I guess there's not much more to say."

Kiki gulped. So he really did confess. "May I see him, sir?"

"Are you sure you want to? As much as I want to believe otherwise, Kiki, he is a murderer."

"Yes, sir, I'm sure."

Sheriff Rodriguez looked Kiki in the eye. "Well, you certainly have the right to visit. That is, if he'll see you. Which I doubt. Carlos hasn't spoken a word to anyone since making his confession. I think he's very confused and angry. He wouldn't see the others. I'll go tell him you're here." The sheriff opened the door, which led to a dimly lit, narrow hallway.

"Please tell him it's important." Who else wanted to see him? she wondered.

The sheriff returned, a surprised look on his face. He motioned to the open door. "End of the hall on your left. But I can't unlock the cell for you. You'll have to talk to him through the bars."

"Thank you, Sheriff," Kiki said. She could see a pale light coming from the room at the end of the hall. Kiki could feel her stomach tightening as she walked down the hall to Spike's cell. A row of vertical steel bars separated the room from the hallway.

"Hi, Spike." Kiki's voice quavered as she spoke to him through the bars. Spike sat with his back to Kiki, on the edge of a narrow cot. The tiny cubicle also contained a white porcelain sink and toilet, and one small, wire-mesh window that looked out on the back of the police station. A bare bulb hung from a fixture from the ceiling, casting a dingy, weak light. Spike

17

was hunched over, his head buried in his hands. Kiki shuddered. It was worse than the movies.

"Spike?" No response. Kiki felt nervous. She wanted to leave, but a voice inside told her to try a little harder. "I want to help you, Spike." He didn't react. "At the cemetery yesterday, when you let them take you in, I thought you were innocent. I want to believe that still." Kiki waited for a reply, but he remained quiet.

"Spike, I don't understand your confession. Who did you lie to? Me or the police?" Kiki demanded. Still nothing. "Why won't you look at me, Spike? Is it because you killed April?"

"No!" Spike shouted. He jumped to his feet and whirled around to face Kiki. "Don't say that. Not you, too."

"Then you didn't do it?"

"I loved her." Spike leaned against the cement wall by the window. He was fighting to control himself. Watching him shaking, his strong body trembling, Kiki could sense all the fear and sadness inside him. So cool, yet so scared.

She knelt down on the floor and pressed her face close to the bars. "The papers say you confessed to killing April."

He nodded.

"But you didn't kill her. You're not making sense, Spike."

"Everything's stacked against me. My lawyer said

that if I confessed, it might get me a lighter sentence." Spike's deep-set dark eyes pleaded for her to understand. "In their eyes, I'm worthless. A lowlife Mexican. That's the way it is in this world."

"But what about the law? If you didn't kill her, you wouldn't have to go to jail. You're innocent," Kiki said.

"But *they* say I'm guilty. My lawyer doesn't even believe me. So how could I prove it to the other side? Who's going to believe Spike Navarrone?" Despair cut deep lines in his face. "They don't care who killed April. As long as someone pays for the crime, they're happy."

"But Sheriff Rodriguez wouldn't falsely convict you just because you're Mexican. He's Mexican."

"It's not the sheriff, Kiki. They brought in federal agents to question me. They grilled me for twelve hours. They *told* me I was guilty. After a while they had me believing it. They said that Hope found the evidence in our secret place. I don't know how she found out where it was. Maybe April told her once."

"But the wrench didn't even have your fingerprints on it, Spike," Kiki said. According to the police reports, the wrench had a fragment of April's hair on it, but was completely free of prints.

"That's because it wasn't mine." Spike threw his arms up in the air in frustration. He started pacing. "It doesn't matter, Kiki. No one believes me. So I'm guilty. I'm going to pay for someone else's crime, just

19

like my father. My dad didn't do anything more than wait in a getaway car. Just so we could eat. And the real criminal? Scot-free."

Kiki saw Spike's anger building up. She pulled herself up to her feet and tried to reason with him. "But if you have proof, then . . ."

Spike came to the front of his cell and grabbed hold of the bars. He looked deep into Kiki's eyes. "It's hopeless. Understand? I'm finished."

Kiki studied his handsome, deeply-troubled face and soft brown eyes, noticing the proud thrust of his jaw as he struggled to control its quivering. What she felt wasn't the end of something, but the beginning . . . a tiny spark flickering to life inside her . . . a new sense of closeness to Spike.

"Spike, I can't just stand by and watch them throw away the key."

Spike frowned. "Then I'll tell you what I told them," he said. He looked at the floor. "I'm guilty."

But Kiki knew why he couldn't meet her eye. He wasn't a killer and they both knew it. "Spike, we've got to fight it," Kiki persisted.

"Look, Kiki." Spike shrugged. "It's over. Drop it." He took a deep breath and exhaled loudly. "I'm sorry, Kiki. It means a lot to me that you care. You're not like everyone else who wanted to see me. Willa Flicker. Some jerk from KPOP. Someone even came from a weekly magazine trying to interview me for a cover story. It's disgusting. April's death isn't gossip."

20

"So you just sent them away?"

Spike nodded. "You know, you're going to get a lot of flak for coming here." Spike gave a bitter laugh. "Pretty funny, actually. The most popular girl in town visits the least popular guy. I like that. Hey, I almost forgot. Congratulations on winning the contest."

"Thanks," Kiki said. She knew it must be hard for Spike to see someone else win the crown that April was supposed to have worn. But he managed a smile for her anyway.

"Spike, do you remember that time when all those guys from San Pedro were bothering me on the green, in front of the town hall?"

"Yeah, I remember that." Spike nodded.

"I'll never forget how you rode up on your motorcycle, completely out of nowhere, and told them that if they ever came near me again, they'd have to answer to you. I was scared out of my mind, but you were so calm and confident. I felt safe with you."

"And now you think you owe me?"

"I think that you owe it to yourself, Spike."

Spike shook his head slightly.

"And what about the real killer? He's still on the loose. There's someone roaming free who murdered April," Kiki protested.

"No!" Spike shouted. He pounded his fist hard against the steel bars. "That bastard!" His eyes were

21

on fire. "Crazy maniac. If I ever get my hands on that bastard, I'll, I'll . . ."

"You'll what, Spike?" Kiki asked. "Kill him? You can't even say the words."

There was a long pause. Spike's pacing slowed. He sank back onto his cot. He looked up at Kiki. "Don't worry about me, Kiki. I'll be fine."

"I'm sorry if I upset you, Spike. Maybe I'd better go." Kiki gave him one last, hopeful glance, but Spike looked away. She turned and started for the door.

"Kiki," Spike said quietly.

"Yes?" Kiki felt a glimmer of hope as she turned back around to look at him. His eyes were so intense. And he was so handsome.

"I need you to do a favor for me."

"Of course. What is it?"

"My little brothers. Would you go check up on them for me? They're out at the trailer."

"They must be terrified."

Spike looked worried, then he actually grinned. "Tell them to stay cool, and hands off my Harley. And . . . tell them their big bro is innocent."

"I promise," Kiki whispered, a lump forming in her throat. "You sure you won't fight it, Spike?"

Spike shook his head. "Yeah, I'm sure. But I have one more favor to ask."

"What's that?" Kiki asked.

"Don't waste any more time worrying about me.

You're the Peach Blossom Queen. Smile. For me, Kiki. You have a beautiful smile," he added softly.

Kiki felt her heart skip a beat. She didn't know what to say. She did smile—shyly but happily. And Spike smiled back—a real, genuine smile, even from behind the prison bars. It was a precious feeling. The bars seemed to disappear for a moment.

But the moment was all too brief. Kiki turned away so Spike wouldn't see the tear trickling down her cheek.

CHAPTER 3

Raven Cruz wiped down the counter of Rosa's Café. You deserved to lose the Peach Blossom contest, she thought, disgusted with herself. Losing the college scholarship that went with the crown meant that Raven's ticket out of Paradiso—attending Stanford in the fall—was lost.

But Raven knew exactly why she had been ignored by the committee. She'd let everyone down. Everybody except Calvin Pinkerton. She couldn't forget the disappointment on the faces of the other SCAM members when she'd suddenly quit. She'd offered all kinds of excuses—her mother's illness, the pressures of schoolwork on top of waitressing nearly full time at her family's restaurant, the fact that SCAM seemed close to losing anyway.

And everybody knew about her huge fight with Vaughn Cutter. Raven felt a hollow ache. She hated to admit to herself how much she missed him. She hadn't mentioned Vaughn at the SCAM meeting, but she knew all the kids had added him to her list of excuses. They'd be horrified to know the real reason she'd dropped out.

Raven thought about the envelope hidden in the basement in the box of toys her brothers and sisters had outgrown. The envelope contained five crisp thousand-dollar bills straight from Lacey's father's safe. How could she ever live with the fact that she'd accepted his money in exchange for quitting her fight against the mall?

She looked out the window of the café at the scrublands. The tall grasses and low, wind-stunted trees shimmered in the clear, soft daylight. Senator Miller had said that saving the scrublands would be almost hopeless without the strong student coalition that had started the battle. Soon Raven would have to live with the knowledge that all this beauty had been destroyed because of her. She had traded the green of nature for the green of dollars. She had sacrificed everything she believed in. But with Mama sick, and no money to pay her medical bills, what was Raven supposed to do? Mama could die!

Still, Raven imagined the songs of the birds in the scrublands, the faint rustling of jackrabbits hopping through the undergrowth, the haunting hoot of the owl you could sometimes hear around sunset. Would all the animals perish to make room for the mall?

"Raven, order up," her sister Carlotta called from the kitchen.

Raven tossed down the cloth she'd been wiping the counter with and picked up the two plates of food Carlotta had prepared. She carried them over to the Carters, at the corner table. Beef Burrito Supreme for Mr. Carter, Taco Salad for Mrs. Carter.

"Everything okay at the pharmacy?" Raven asked politely as she put their dinners down in front of them. "Hot plate, Mr. Carter. Careful, now."

"Aren't you nice for asking," Mrs. Carter said. "Business is just fine. And how are *you*, dear?" Raven knew that she had heard the news about the Peach Blossom Queen.

Raven almost resented kindly, round-faced Mrs. Carter for her sympathy. It was hard to know that everyone in town was looking at her and thinking, "Poor Raven." Especially since the Peach Blossom crown itself meant so little to her. In fact, she was happy that Kiki would be wearing it. Her new friendship with Kiki was the one good thing that had come out of the mess of the past weeks. Still, Kiki didn't need that scholarship half as much as Raven did.

But as the bell over the café door jingled and Papa marched in, Raven was reminded that she had more immediate problems than college. Papa's face was twisted into a dark, pained scowl.

"Raven," he called to her, motioning her over.

Raven rushed toward him. "Papa?"

26

"There is a Dr. Joseph at the house who says he has been sent to treat Mama," Papa said in Spanish.

Raven nodded. "I know."

"And you also know that we have no insurance to pay for his visit." It was a statement, not a question.

Raven looked at the floor. "Don't worry about it, Papa," she said. "I'll take care of it."

"You'll take care of it," Papa echoed in disbelief. "Have you discovered buried treasure behind the chicken coop?"

Raven swallowed hard. "Papa, a—a friend is helping Mama."

Papa was silent for a moment. Then he asked, "Your friend, Vaughn, who drives the expensive car?"

Raven bit her lip. Papa and Vaughn had gotten on just fine. Then she and Vaughn had driven up to the Cutters' cabin and accidentally fallen asleep in front of the fire. They hadn't come home until the next afternoon. Now Vaughn was about as far from Papa's good graces as he could get.

"No, Papa. You don't have to worry about me and Vaughn Cutter anymore," Raven spat. She thought about how angry she'd been at Vaughn for bowing to his parents' demands and leaving SCAM. She remembered the ugly words they had hurled at each other outside the café, and the way Vaughn's famous temper had exploded. She remembered him pummeling the wire mesh of the chicken coop, blood on his hands. The image still haunted her. But what scared

27

her more was that now she'd sacrificed her own prin-
ciples and quit SCAM—just what she'd been furious
at Vaughn for doing.

"Well, if the money's not Vaughn's," Papa demanded, "then where is this instant wealth coming
from?"

Raven shrugged miserably. "Papa, please don't ask
me any more questions," she whispered. "I can't tell
you who's paying the doctor bills, but it's okay. I
promise."

Papa's face said it wasn't. "Raven, I have never
taken charity in my life," he said. "And I don't want
to see you doing it, either."

"It's not charity, Papa." That was true. It was
worse. It was a bribe.

CHAPTER 4

Hope Hubbard stared at the screen of her computer, but she couldn't concentrate on the columns of numbers and symbols. The ache she felt from missing April wouldn't go away. She pulled open the right-hand drawer of her desk and took out the sketch she'd tucked away. She was drawn in soft pencil lines, tall, skinny and dark haired, standing next to April, curvy, if not a little plump, her hair in wild red curls —Hope supplied the fiery color in her mind. Both girls were grinning. *To Hope, Love always, Your cousin, April,* it said under the drawing.

Always, Hope thought, swallowing hard. Always had not turned out to be very long for April. She studied the drawing, remembering how she'd watched April sketch as they'd sat on the front steps of school. Hope sighed and put the picture back in the drawer. She hoped one day she'd be able to take it out and frame it, and hang it on her wall. But it

29

was still too painful. And the bitter feud between Hope's mother and April's father wouldn't permit it. The family battle had not died with April.

Far from it. Uncle Ward had even gone to the sheriff and suggested that Hope might be involved in the murder. Hope tried to understand. She knew Uncle Ward and Aunt Sara had to be grieving for their only child even more than she was. She could only pray that Uncle Ward's hysterical accusations would stop now that April's murderer was behind bars.

Hope let out a long sigh. She still had trouble believing that Spike Navarrone really was the killer. Hope had been convinced that Spike loved April. But there had been April's note, telling Spike to meet her at their secret spot the night of the murder. As soon as bigmouthed Penny Bolton thought she had found the place, she spread it all around school. Hope had gone down to investigate and found the murder weapon, a gleaming wrench half-buried under the tree.

She picked up the math text from the little pile of books and magazines near her computer—Spike's books and magazines. He'd asked her to get them for him from his school locker, then he'd disappeared before Hope could give them back. She flipped open the math book. CARLOS NAVARRONE, it said, in capital letters. Under it was a big heart. C. N. + A. L. Hope had found the same thing in most of Spike's books. "Spike loves April." Had it all been the most

30

twisted, elaborate charade? Or had some awful accident taken place under that ponderosa tree?

Hope slammed the book shut. The grisly facts were that Spike had been caught. And he'd confessed. Hope left her computer blinking at her, and went and flopped down on her bed. She'd thought that finding her cousin's murderer would be a relief. Instead she felt confused and frightened. The boy her cousin had loved had turned out to be some kind of monster. You couldn't count on anything. Not even your deepest feelings about a person.

Hope thought about Jess—about his strong swimmer's arms, and his sensitive, caring blue eyes. She thought about how he made her laugh and how easy it was to talk to him. She thought about the way he kissed. Her heart raced just thinking about it. They were getting closer every day. But did she know him as well as she thought she did?

Just this afternoon, down by the quarry on the edge of town, Jess had told her she had to try to put the murder behind her now.

"I'm not telling you to forget April," he'd said as they'd dangled their feet in the cool water. "But you've gotta accept what happened and move on. I don't know. Maybe this sounds weird, but I think you have to get the most out of life—for April and for you."

Hope appreciated Jess's concern. And the long, sweet kisses he'd given her to try to cheer her up. But

31

Hope couldn't break free of the sadness that gripped her.

It seemed that something as brutally ugly as murder could breed only more ugliness. Hope squeezed her eyes shut, as if she could block out her own thoughts. The doorbell startled her. Hope's eyes popped open, and she got up to answer the door.

Kiki De Santis was on her doorstep. "The new Peggy Sue!" Hope said, surprised. She and Kiki were friendly with each other, but they had never hung out much outside of school. She wondered why the Queen of Paradiso had come to visit. "Hey, congratulations, Kiki!"

"Thanks," Kiki said. But she looked more upset than happy.

"Is something wrong?" Hope asked. "You want to come in?"

Kiki nodded. "If it's okay. I know it's kind of late. . . ."

"No problem," Hope said. "My mom's still at work. Late shift at the hospital. I was just trying to do my math homework. And failing."

"You?" Kiki said. "Hope Hubbard, computer whiz? I don't believe it."

"Calculus." Hope shrugged. She let Kiki in and led the way to her room. "Couldn't concentrate. I was thinking about April."

Kiki sat down on the edge of Hope's bed. "Hope, that's why I'm here."

"April?" Hope asked.

Kiki nodded. "Spike didn't kill her."

Hope sat down in her rocking chair and let out a loud sigh. "Kiki, I didn't want to believe it, either. I still don't want to. But we have to face it. Spike even said he did it. That's the final proof, isn't it?"

Kiki shook her head vehemently. "I just visited him in jail. He says he was pressured into confessing by some federal agents. He's sure he's going to be found guilty no matter what, and that he'll get a lighter sentence if he tells them what they want to hear."

Hope was stunned. She brought her hands to her face and tried to make sense out of what Kiki was saying. "He's innocent, but he confessed?"

Kiki nodded. "He looked terrible. I mean, for Spike," she added.

Hope heard warning bells going off. She studied Kiki carefully. Was she blushing? "Wait a minute, Kiki. Can we take it back a few steps?" she asked. "Why did you go visit Spike Navarrone in the first place? He's a confessed killer."

Kiki toyed with a strand of her long, chocolate-brown hair. "You know I was with Spike when they came to get him?"

Hope nodded. "I read it in the *Record*. You were bringing flowers to April's grave, only Spike got there first."

"For once, Willa Flicker was right," Kiki said.

33

"But what she doesn't know is that we heard the sirens way before the sheriff showed up. Spike could have gotten away. He actually did start to run. But Hope, I told him that if he was innocent, he should stay and defend himself."

"And he stopped running."

Kiki nodded. "I was sure he was all set to fight the charges. Then when he confessed, well, I just had to hear him tell it to my face. Except he couldn't. Because he's innocent. All I had to do was look into his eyes, and I knew he didn't do it. I believe him, Hope." Kiki's voice got dreamy and faraway.

"Kiki, you know April fell awfully hard for Spike too," Hope said guardedly. She'd seen Spike Navarrone work his charms on her cousin. And now her cousin was dead.

"Hope, I'm not falling for Spike," Kiki protested.

"You're not?"

Kiki traced imaginary patterns in Hope's bedspread. "Well—maybe a little."

Hope leaned forward in her rocking chair. "Kiki, aren't you still dating Bobby?" Then she realized what she was saying. "What about the fact that Spike's a murderer?"

"He's not," Kiki said. "I'd bet my life on it."

"Don't even say that, Kiki." It was weird, thinking about Spike and someone besides April. Weird and creepy. Spike's love might be a death sentence.

Kiki shrugged her shoulders. "But I know he's not

34

the killer. And the only way to prove it is to find out who really did kill April. That's why I came to you. The sheriff can't reopen the case since he has Spike's confession. Don't you see? He's trapped."

"And you want me to help him?" Hope asked.

"Hope, you're the smartest person in Paradiso High. Well, except maybe for Winston Purdy."

Hope waved her hand.

"I'm serious, Hope," Kiki pleaded. "I need your help. I know you were trying to find the murderer before Spike got arrested."

Hope hesitated. She thought of what Jess had said about putting the murder behind her. Reopening the case would be as painful as it would be difficult, not to mention dangerous.

"At least come out and visit Spike's brothers with me," Kiki said. "I told him I'd look in on them. Please, Hope. I suppose I could command you as your Queen," she added, giving a desperate-sounding half laugh.

"You don't have to do that," Hope said. "I almost forgot about Spike's brothers. With Mrs. Navarrone out drinking at the Blue Hawaii all the time, I wonder who's going to take care of them now. I'll go out there with you. Tomorrow after school?"

"Great," Kiki said. "I knew I could count on you."

Hope thought of something and shuddered. "Just one request, Kiki. Don't tell anyone, okay? If Spike turns out to be innocent, that means the killer is still out there. I don't want anyone to know I'm looking for clues again."

Hope couldn't forget the warning on the school computer telling her to stay out of the search for April's killer. Even more terrifying was the memory of being chased through the woods, rocks whizzing by her like deadly missiles. Was it the real killer who had tried to scare her off the case—maybe scare her to death? If Spike Navarrone wasn't the murderer, then Hope was still in danger.

CHAPTER 5

It was practically midnight when Lacey pulled her Ferrari into the driveway. She had been driving for hours. Alone. Fast and furiously through parts of Sacramento Valley that she hadn't even known existed. Anywhere but Paradiso. Lacey needed to get the Peach Blossom contest out of her head, and doing ninety miles an hour with the top down was the best way she knew. But now that she was back in Paradiso, she could feel the weight of depression returning.

Lacey had hoped her parents would be asleep when she got home. But she could see from outside that the lights were on throughout the house. As if she didn't feel bad enough already for losing, now her parents were going to make her feel even worse.

She sat in her car, wanting to put off her confrontation with them for as long as she could. Or avoid it altogether. *I should turn right around and split.* She looked inside at the house, all lit up by crystal chandeliers and adorned with elaborate wall sconces. Precious art objects filled every room. Everything anybody could possibly want was inside there—except happiness. Lacey felt more comfortable outside. Alone, in the dark. But she knew she couldn't stay away forever. She'd have to face her parents sooner or later. Get it over with, babe, she told herself. Get it over with so you can start forgetting it as soon as possible.

Lacey made her way up the steps and let herself into the house. She found Mother exactly as she had expected. Darla was completely predictable. She sat in the living room on the white couch, wedged against the armrest. Dressed completely in black, she sipped her drink. Her head held tight and her body rocking slightly, she stared glassy eyed at the front door. Mother always faced the door. She always seemed on the verge of bolting.

Lacey tried to ignore her and headed straight for her room. She had taken only the first step up the staircase when Darla's icy voice made her stop. "Come here," she ordered.

Trapped. "Yes, Mother." Lacey came as far as the entranceway to the living room. I'm gonna be just as cold as you, Lacey decided. No way was she going to break down and be intimidated. "I'm tired, Mother. I need my beauty sleep. Good night."

"Beauty?" Darla's stare kept an evil hold on Lacey.

They looked at each other for a long, ugly moment. Not a hint of compassion from her own mother.

Lacey took in a deep breath of air and tried to exhale all the tension. "It wasn't my fault, Mother. I should have won."

"But you didn't." Darla turned her head away as if she was ashamed even to look at a loser. "It's humiliating." Her disapproval showed in every wretched contortion.

Lacey had promised herself she'd remain strong, but her head felt hot and she fought to hold back tears. "I know I let you down. Like always," Lacey said bitterly.

Mother nodded in agreement.

Lacey wanted to slap her. "Fine. Be that way. But you know what? I don't care." She tried to believe her own words.

"You're damn right you don't," Darla snapped, "or you would have won. Instead you let Kiki De Santis beat you. Kiki De Santis!"

The tears started to flow. "I tried! Did you hear me, Mother? I said I tried. I tried, damn it. Won't you listen to me?" But not a word from Mother.

Just a long, cold silence.

"Darla, great news!" Daddy's voice rang out from upstairs. "That was Standish on the phone from Sacramento," he shouted, his voice getting louder as he made his way down the stairs. "He's got a meeting scheduled with the zoning board early next week. He says we're a signature away. We're gonna have a mall!" he exclaimed.

He came into the living room and scooped Lacey up from behind, his big hands clamped around her tiny waist, lifting her high in the air. "We're gonna have a mall, we're gonna have a mall, Lacey!"

But as he brought Lacey down, his smile disappeared. "You're crying! Princess, what's the matter?" He patted the top of her head, brushing back her hair. "Shhh, what is it?"

"I'm sorry, Daddy. I didn't mean to lose the contest," Lacey sobbed. The tears froze with fear as she saw the deep frown forming on Daddy's rugged face. He was wearing a navy pinstripe suit with the suspenders she'd given him for Christmas. He looked so handsome and distinguished, his newly-barbered hair streaked with silver, gold cufflinks twinkling at his wrists.

"Shhh. It's okay, princess." He wrapped his arms around her and pulled her close. "Shhh," he whispered in her ear. "Daddy still thinks you're a winner."

Lacey looked up at him. "You mean you don't hate me? You don't think I'm a failure?" She looked into her father's eyes, trying to find the anger. But it wasn't there. Instead she saw compassion. Real, live sympathy.

"Lacey, you're my precious princess. If you lost,

40

it's only because you're too good for the rest of Paradiso."

Lacey looked up at him. "You mean it, Daddy?"

Calvin kissed her forehead.

"You're the best. I love you," Lacey said, giving him a big hug. Something was seriously different about Daddy. She could feel it. He didn't even smell like liquor. Daddy hadn't had a drop. Could things possibly be changing around here?

Calvin eyed Darla coldly. "Did your mother say how sorry she was that you lost the contest, Lacey?" he asked. "Did you, Darla?"

"Of course I did, Calvin," Darla muttered, her eyes darting away from them.

"I see," Calvin said, his voice tight with disbelief. He turned back to Lacey. She was still shaking. "Princess, I have a great idea. Are you hungry?"

"Hungry?" Food hadn't exactly been the biggest thing on Lacey's mind.

"Well, I'm starved. I've been working since seven o'clock this morning on the mall project, and I've barely eaten all day. Remember that great Chinese restaurant that's open all night? The one with the amazing shrimp in black bean sauce?"

"And the delicious noodles?" Lacey's stomach began to rumble. "But it's in San Francisco," Lacey reminded him.

"Never stopped us before, did it?" Daddy said with a grin. "I don't think we can land the jet in

41

Chinatown, but we'll see about bringing the chopper down."

She felt a huge smile stretching across her face. "What are we waiting for?" She wasn't quite sure what to make of his good mood, but she decided she'd better enjoy it while she could.

"Come on, princess," Daddy said as he headed for the door. "I can taste it already."

Lacey turned to Darla, who remained glued to the couch, speechless. "Don't wait up for us, Mother," she said.

Thank goodness I'm out of there. For a little while, anyway, Lacey thought as she slammed the door behind her. Mother thought she was a loser, and maybe everyone in Paradiso did too. But at least to Daddy she was still someone special.

As Lacey and Daddy walked hand in hand to the helicopter, she prayed that her black eye and bruised legs could finally heal once and for all.

CHAPTER 6

"That's right, Lacey dear. Oops, I mean, Kiki dear," Miss Crane said. This was the second time Miss Crane had mistaken Kiki for Lacey. "Straight ahead. Two more steps. Good. Now, here's where you make your curtsy to Mr. Appleby and the rest of the committee."

Two rows of chairs were set up onstage to form a makeshift aisle for the rehearsal. Kiki walked between the chairs, keeping her head high. She tried walking the entire path without knocking into anything. She knew she was supposed to maintain her poise—a queen's posture—by keeping her body straight and focused forward. But she couldn't help putting her hands up to her head every so often to make sure the cardboard crown she was practicing with stayed on. Which it didn't. She'd been rehearsing for an hour and still hadn't managed to make it through once without doing something wrong.

43

She made another attempt. Two graceful, queen-like strides, the way she'd been shown by Miss Crane.

"Not such long, lanky steps, dear. Dainty. Dainty."

Kiki threw her hands up in the air in frustration, sending the crown to the ground. "I'll never get it right. It's impossible," she lamented as she knelt to pick up the crown.

"That's because you're so uncoordinated," Lacey muttered to herself. As runner-up, Lacey had to be at every rehearsal. Until that comment, she and Kiki hadn't exchanged a single word. Which was fine with Kiki. But now Lacey was going into gear.

Kiki wondered why Lacey was participating in the ceremony at all. Normally if Lacey didn't get her way with something, she had nothing to do with it. She was probably still waiting for Kiki to drop out. Fat chance, Kiki thought.

"Better make sure your sneakers are double-knotted on the day of the Festival," Lacey remarked dryly. "The polka-dotted ones will go great with your ball gown."

"Lay off, Lacey," Kiki snapped, adjusting the crown. She had known it was just a matter of time before Lacey would start causing trouble. It was her middle name.

"Now, now, Kiki, relax. It just takes patience," Miss Crane, math teacher and self-appointed etiquette coach, comforted her. Kiki couldn't believe

Miss Crane had totally ignored Lacey's nasty remarks. She always seemed to give Lacey the benefit of the doubt. In math class and here, too.

Kiki took another step, but the crown dropped off immediately. "Darn."

"It's not going to be easy, dear. You're doing just fine," Miss Crane said, a touch of hesitation in her voice. "Every year it's the same." Miss Crane was an institution at Paradiso High—her tall, bony figure as familiar a sight as the ancient bell on the front lawn. She had been a student there years ago, graduating in the same class with Calvin Pinkerton.

"Is this where I wave?" Kiki felt silly for asking. I can't believe I have to be told when to wave. I thought this was going to be a little more natural. She never realized that being Peach Blossom Queen would be so demanding. There were a million things to learn, and she had just begun. One right way to do everything. And a million wrong ways. A Queen had to act just so. It seemed to Kiki that she was being transformed into someone else—an even mixture of fairy-tale princess and Miss Manners.

"Let's try it again, from the beginning," Miss Crane said, her pale, rabbity eyes flickering with impatience despite her calm tone. "Now relax, and *try* to remember what we just went over." The math teacher cast a regretful glance at Lacey, as if she were wishing it was Lacey in Kiki's place.

Miss Crane wasn't the only one who felt that way.

45

As Kiki walked to the back of the stage to start over, she caught Lacey's cold stare. It still felt weird to Kiki being the one on a pedestal, looking down on Lacey. It had always been the other way around, from the time they were little. Kiki asking for Lacey's approval, obeying Lacey's commands. Finally, things were different. Kiki was the star, the winner, no matter how many times she dropped her crown or forgot to wave.

She started slowly down the aisle. Let's see. Straight ahead. Smile. The crown is on your head. There's Lacey's trying to make a fool of me. "Shoot!" Kiki crashed into a chair, knocking it to the floor. "I'm sorry," she said, turning beet red.

"Kiki dear," Miss Crane clicked her tongue, "remember that those chairs represent people. Think of those seats as your loyal subjects and well-wishers. They will be rooting you on. You wouldn't want to bump into them or trip over anybody, would you?"

"Queen Klutz," Lacey muttered.

A few laughs came from the balcony. Kiki looked up, but it was too dark to make out any faces. She had an idea who was up there, though. Lacey's loyal troops, no doubt.

"Miss Crane, does Lacey have to be here while I practice?" she asked, frustration rising in her voice. "She's making me nervous."

"I'll split if you want. I don't need this," Lacey said, reaching for her bag.

Miss Crane walked over to Lacey. "Lacey, sweetie, please stay."

"But Raven's not here," Lacey protested.

I wish she were. Instead of you, Kiki thought. We'd be having a ball up here.

"Raven will only be called upon should something prevent both you and Kiki from accepting the crown," Miss Crane explained, putting a motherly arm around her, "but for now, you are lady-in-waiting, and it's your duty to learn everything. Just in case. You'd wear the crown if something were to happen to Miss De Santis."

"If something happened to Miss De Santis, she'd deserve it," Lacey cracked.

Kiki felt a shot of fear.

"Don't give me that stupid look, Kiki," Lacey snapped. "You have nothing to worry about. The murderer is behind bars. So you're safe and sound. Nothing's gonna happen to your precious royal self."

But the murderer's not in jail. Not as far as I'm concerned, Kiki thought. She noted Lacey's menacing glare. Lacey was just like her mother, Darla. Kiki felt cold. Was Lacey sitting pretty in the runner-up's seat, just a murder away from being Queen?

No, Kiki was certain that the murderer wasn't in jail at all. Her thoughts turned to Spike. Another day in that horrible cell, keeping all his thoughts locked up inside him. She pictured him sitting on his cot, staring blankly out his cell window. Suddenly being

Peach Blossom Queen seemed so unimportant. How could she worry about walking right, smiling right, and waving right, when Spike might never be free again?

"Miss Crane, haven't we done enough for one day? It's still more than a week till the Festival," Kiki said. She couldn't wait to get out to the trailer with Hope and make sure Spike's brothers were okay. Maybe she'd have time to go to see Spike afterward.

But Miss Crane shook her head. "Kiki, we've barely gotten past your entrance. We still have to rehearse your ride down Old Town Road on the float, and the speech you'll make at the podium. And we haven't even gotten to your duties at the fair and at the ball. It's all so important. Young lady, no one said it would be easy being a Queen."

Kiki was ready to scream. "I thought this was going to be fun! This is worse than final exams," she said.

"What a dork." Lacey chuckled.

"Now, Lacey," Miss Crane said mildly. She came over to Kiki. "I know this is hard for you, dear. Every one of my Peach Blossom girls in the past has gone through exactly the same thing. But on the day of the Festival, when you're looking so elegant in your flowing gown, the jeweled crown so regal in your hair, well . . ." Her eyes teared up. She was *so* weird. "All your friends and family will be smiling, so happy for

48

you, and, well—I just can't describe how wonderful you're going to feel."

Kiki took a deep breath and nodded. Maybe it just took a little more practice. She *was* the Queen, and she was going to have a blast at the Festival. And everybody was going to be proud of her. Everyone. Including Spike, if she had her way. Kiki was going to prove his innocence. And she'd do it before the Festival. She pictured him waiting for her at the end of the parade. Free.

"Okay, Miss Crane, I'm ready to try again." Kiki went back to the beginning of the aisle. She gave Lacey a little wink. Very humble servant, she thought, giggling to herself.

"Ready, dear?" Miss Crane asked. "Like it counts."

Kiki glided down the aisle gracefully. Light as a feather. In her head she imagined the band, ten wide and twenty deep, marching behind her. Trumpets blaring, drums beating loudly. Thousands faithfully cheering. And Spike. Spike!

"That's it, good! Marvelous," Miss Crane exclaimed as Kiki continued.

Kiki whirled around, making the first wave to where Mr. Appleby would be standing. Smiling brightly, she curtsied to the rest of the Peach Blossom committee, then waved again to the townspeople. She continued down the aisle, turned to where the float would be waiting for the Queen's arrival, and ascended the makeshift steps, two wooden benches. Then, with a giant smile, she waved to the most important person of all. Spike Navarrone.

Miss Crane clapped loudly for Kiki. "Kiki dear, I think the Queen of England could take a few lessons from you."

"That really was fun. Thanks for being so patient, Miss Crane."

"That's what I'm here for. I'm glad you're starting to enjoy it. Let's call it a day. We'll stop on a good note. Now, don't forget that feeling, Kiki. That marvelous feeling that only a Queen knows. See you tomorrow. And you too, Lacey," she said. Kiki glanced over at Lacey's chair, but it was empty. "Lacey?" Miss Crane said quizzically. Seeing that Lacey wasn't anywhere, Miss Crane's thin face seemed to sag with disappointment. Talk about teacher's pet!

Kiki was walking on air as she left the auditorium. Maybe it really was going to be great. But her high spirits plummeted back to earth when she saw Bobby in the school lobby.

"Hi, Keeks," he said, planting a kiss on her cheek.

"Bobby? What are you doing here?" Kiki asked.

"You were great, Kiki. I'm really lucky. Me, with the Queen. You looked so beautiful onstage."

Kiki felt a stab of guilt. Why did he have to be so nice?

"Want to go for an ice cream or something? A banana royale for the Queen?"

50

"Bobby . . . I . . . Well, I . . ." Just then she saw Hope coming through the door. Rescued. Bobby was looking at her with puppy-dog eyes. "I can't, Bobby. I'm really sorry. I have plans."

"Can I call you tonight?" he asked. "I'd love to spend a little time with you. We still haven't celebrated your winning yet."

"We will, Bobby. Promise." Even the Queen lies, she thought. And even the Queen can feel super guilty. "I gotta go, Bobby. I'll see you."

Straight ahead, don't look back, she told herself as she went for the exit, leaving Bobby staring after her. Hope followed.

They ran smack into Penny Bolton on the steps of the school.

"Hi, Queenie," Penny said, with a fake brightness, curtsying in her tennis whites. "Nice performance. I saw the whole thing from the balcony."

"I figured that was you up there. I know you think Lacey should be the Queen."

"Should be, and might be," Penny said, raising an eyebrow.

Kiki shot Penny a hard stare. "You know, Penny, you can really be a jerk sometimes. With all that's happened in the past few weeks, couldn't you have a little more class?"

"I'm just telling you for your own good, Kiki. If that's the way you thank me for the favor, well, forget

51

it. I'll see you around. I hope," she said, and walked off. Penny could really ham it up when she wanted to.

Kiki was furious. "I can't believe that little rat."

"Don't worry, Kiki. She's just trying to get your goat. I think we both know who puts her up to all her moves. Lacey will try just about anything."

Kiki frowned. "That's what I'm afraid of."

CHAPTER 7

"That's where I got chased," Hope pointed out to Kiki. Kiki steered her parents' Isuzu Trooper down the long road that cut through the woods to the Navarrones' trailer. "If Jess hadn't gotten there in time, I don't know what would have happened." She shuddered.

"Totally creepy," Kiki said.

Hope nodded. She touched her face where the rock had grazed her skin, even though the wound had healed. She couldn't help thinking about how this was awfully close to where Spike lived. Everyone thought Spike had left town after the murder, but it turned out he'd been sleeping in an abandoned car near the trailer so he could keep an eye on his brothers. Since Spike had been in Paradiso all along, Hope thought, he could have been the one who had chased her.

But she didn't say anything to Kiki. She knew Kiki

was a hundred percent convinced of Spike's innocence. Hope wanted to believe Kiki was right.

Kiki pulled the Trooper into the Navarrones' front yard—or what would have been a front yard in someone else's home. It was little more than a clearing in the woods, with the trailer on cinder blocks behind it. And there was the car Spike had been sleeping in—a rusted hunk of metal not far from the trailer. Spike's mom really had to be dead drunk all the time not to know her son had been camping out there.

Spike's two little brothers were bent over a beat-up BMX bicycle, doing something to the seat. As Kiki pulled alongside them, they both looked up warily.

"Hey, guys," Kiki said cheerfully as she shut off the motor. "Let's see. You're Ricky." She nodded at the older one, a miniature version of Spike, with his dark hair, deep-set eyes, and full mouth. "And you must be Tony."

Hope admired Kiki's easy, friendly manner, the way she could talk and act as if nothing were wrong. No wonder Kiki had been chosen Queen.

"Hi," Ricky said, sounding suspicious. Tony stopped what he was doing and tried to hide behind his brother.

"I'm Kiki, a friend of Spike's," Kiki said in a reassuring way. "And this is Hope."

Hope hopped out of the Trooper. "You guys know me. Remember when I was out here visiting your brother?"

54

"Yeah," Ricky said. He was working at a screw with a long screwdriver. It looked as if he was trying to loosen it, but he didn't seem to be getting very far.

Kiki got out of the driver's side and came around. "Guys, we're here because we have a message from your brother."

Ricky stopped working. "You do?" Now Kiki had his attention.

Little Tony poked his head out from behind Ricky's back. "Spike?" he said.

Kiki nodded. "He loves you very much," she said. "You too, Ricky. He wanted you to know that. And he also wanted you to know that he didn't do what people are saying he did."

"We know that," Ricky said. He sounded as certain as Kiki.

Hope bit her lip. This was not the time or place to voice any doubts.

"He also wanted to know how you guys were getting on," Kiki said. She ruffled little Tony's mop of dark hair. "You guys behaving yourselves?"

Tony nodded solemnly.

"Are you hungry?" Kiki asked.

"I know how to cook some things," Ricky said with a touch of pride. Hope took a good look at Spike's brothers. Ricky looked about eleven. Tony was perhaps seven or eight.

"Are you going to school?" Kiki asked.

Both boys said they were. Hope was impressed

with how polite and well behaved they were. Some-one had done something right with them. And with Mrs. Navarrone camped out at the Blue Hawaii and Mr. Navarrone in jail, that someone had to be Spike. Could a guy like that really be a killer?

Ricky went back to work on the bicycle, straining his arms to unscrew the bolt under the seat. It wouldn't budge.

"What are you trying to do?" Kiki asked.

"Raise the seat," Ricky explained. "Tony's gotten too big for it," he added, taking over Spike's role of big brother.

"Here, want me to try?" Kiki asked. Ricky handed her the screwdriver. "Just like Spike, huh? Always fussing with your bike," she said affectionately. She strained to turn the screw. "It's totally rusted," she said. "Here, Hope. I can't get it. Wanna try?"

Hope took the screwdriver and knelt down in front of the bicycle. Ricky held it for her. She used all her strength against the rusted bolt. Nothing. She paused for a moment, flexing her hands around the slender yellow handle of the tool. She noticed something scratched into the plastic, and took a closer look.

CARLOS NAVARRONE, it said, in crudely etched let-ters. Hope thought about how all the tools in Jess's father's auto shop had "Property of Gardner's Auto Body and Repair" scratched into the metal. The wrench she and Jess had found under Spike and

April's tree was smooth and unaltered. Her heart skipped a beat.

"Ricky, do all your brother's tools have his name on them?" she asked, a tremor of excitement in her voice. She ran her finger over the letters cut into the screwdriver's handle.

Ricky thought for a moment, then shrugged. "I don't know."

"Hope, what is it?" Kiki asked, catching on to Hope's mood. "What's up?"

"This tool is marked," Hope explained. "Just like all of Jess's tools. The wrench the sheriff's holding as the murder weapon doesn't say anything."

Kiki raised a fist in the air. "Yeah! I knew it!"

Hope put a hand on Kiki's arm. "Kiki," she said softly. "We don't know anything for certain. Not yet. Maybe it's just this one that says his name." She turned back to Ricky. "Do you know where Spike keeps the rest of his tools?" she asked.

"Sure," Ricky said. "Under his bed. Mom said there wasn't any room for them anyplace else in the trailer. She said she didn't want to live in a greasy workshop."

"Ricky," she asked gently, "do you think I could take a look at Spike's other tools?"

"You think it will get him out of jail?" he asked, a note of eagerness creeping into his voice.

"I don't know," Hope said. "Maybe."

Ricky and Tony led the way into the Navarrones'

shabby green trailer. Hope and Kiki followed behind. Hope remembered how she'd peered into one of the windows the last time she'd been here and seen Mrs. Navarrone lying passed out on the floor. Fortunately, the boys' mother was nowhere to be found.

There were, however, piles of dishes in the tiny sink, and enough empty bottles and cans on the small table built into one wall of the trailer to start a recycling center. This was the main room, combination kitchen–living room. A bedspread hung as a curtain separated it from the bedroom, a tiny space with just enough room for two sets of bunk beds.

Ricky pulled out from under one of the bunks a wooden box filled with tools. Hope could feel her heart beating as she reached into it. She took out a hammer and inspected it closely. She felt her pulse take off. "C. N." was etched into the metal just above the black-rubber handle covering!

"Kiki, it says his name!" Hope exclaimed. She pulled another tool out of the box, a monkey wrench about the size of the one she'd found under the tree: CARLOS NAVARRONE.

Hope sifted through the box in a frenzy. "All his tools are marked! Oh my God, Kiki, you may be right!"

"Is Spike going to come home?" Tony asked, sensing Hope and Kiki's excitement.

Hope stooped down to look right at Tony. "I hope so," she said seriously. "But you have to promise me not to say anything about this. To *anyone.*" If the real killer found out what she and Kiki suspected, they'd be in grave danger. If they weren't already.

"We won't tell," Tony said. "I promise."

"You guys mind if I take a couple of the tools?" Hope asked them. "To show the sheriff," she explained to Kiki.

Ricky let her put the hammer and the wrench in her shoulder bag.

"Great," Hope said.

"Now you two call me if there are any problems, or if you need anything, okay?" Kiki told the boys. She tore off a piece of the cover from an old magazine that was lying around, and Hope watched her write her phone number out with a stubby, chewed-up pencil Ricky handed her. She fished around in her back pocket and pulled out a couple of quarters. "Save these for phone calls." The Navarrone trailer was not equipped with a telephone.

Ricky put the phone number and the quarters in the corner of Spike's toolbox, and pushed the box back under the bed. "Please get Spike to come home to us," he said shyly.

"We'll do our best," Hope promised.

Hope prayed that they wouldn't be let down— while the real killer went free. It was up to her.

CHAPTER 8

"Really, Lacey," Renée said, shaking her head in bewilderment, her mane of red hair sliding over her shoulders. She stood almost a head taller than Lacey, who peered up at her friend as she spoke. "I think this is the first time in my life that I've been in a clothing store with you when you haven't bought at least one thing. You must really be bumming about this Peggy Sue thing."

"Me? No way. You know me, babe. I don't let these little things get to me." Lacey looked around the Virginia Shoppe, the chic new boutique in town. But she just didn't feel like shopping today. "I just don't want any of this junk. Let's split."

Lacey led the way out of the store. "The rehearsal was a serious drag. I had to sit there like a prisoner and watch Kiki and that old bag Miss Crane make fools of themselves onstage. D-R-A-G, a big drag."

"Yeah, Penny told me. Sounds miserable. I still

can't get over the fact that Kiki beat you," Renée said. "Hey, you feel like walking a little?"

"Sure. Whatever." Lacey and Renée headed down Old Town Road. The sun shone brightly, winking off the hoods of parked cars, and the newly-sprinkled grass of the town green off in the distance. "Believe me, Renée, I'm over the loss."

Renée shot Lacey a skeptical look.

Lacey knew she was failing to convince Renée. But she refused to show her disappointment, even to her closest friends. You wouldn't believe some of the things I'm supposed to do as lady-in-waiting."

"Like what?" Renée asked.

"Like bowing before Kiki in front of the whole town. Me kneeling down to Kiki?" Lacey groaned. "And check this out. I'm supposed to hold the back of her gown up off the floor so it won't get dirty. Some old-fashioned custom."

"So why don't you quit?" Renée asked.

Lacey smirked.

"It's not over till it's over. I heard Kiki was getting tight with Spike. Maybe they'll let him out, and he'll do Kiki in next. Then Raven Cruz can carry *my* train."

"Lacey!" Renée said, "Don't even joke like that."

Lacey shrugged. *"Qué será, será.* Anyway, I'm telling you, Renée, the whole thing stinks. And I think the contest was fixed. Kiki shouldn't have won."

"Seriously?" Renée's eyes were wide.

61

Lacey nodded. "You know all those ugly rumors about my parents and the mall and April? All that Willa Flicker garbage in the *Record*, I mean. After a while I was believing it too," she admitted.

"Yeah, I'm sure it was really tough on you, Lacey. I was really worried for you for a while there. But you think they'd throw the contest because of those rumors?"

"Flicker convinced a lot of people that my family was evil. She made the whole committee turn against me. Why else would they choose Kiki over me?"

"Sure, Lacey, you're probably right," Renée said. "Willa should have written a formal apology. She owes your family that, at least."

"At least," Lacey agreed. "But I guess when you're the number-one family in town, the little people are always out to get you, always trying to put you down. Let Kiki enjoy her throne for a few days. I'll be looking back down at her soon enough."

"Listen, Lacey. You've always been around to help me when I needed it. You know I'm here for you, too."

"Thanks, Renée, but like I said, I'll be fine. Trust me. See, I'm smiling." Lacey manufactured an ear-to-ear grin. She sneaked a look at Renée to see if she believed her. Lacey couldn't stand having her friends think Kiki had gotten the better of her. Especially a nut case like Renée "I Stabbed My Mother with a

62

Barbecue Fork" Henderson. "Really, Renée, you're sweet, but it's just high school stuff, you know?"

They continued along Old Town Road until they came to the town green. They stopped to sit on the bench at the edge of the lawn. As much as Lacey refused to admit it, she couldn't get Kiki and the contest out of her mind. It was killing Lacey to think that Kiki had everyone fussing over her. Soon she'd be leading the parade right past this very spot. And Lacey would be behind her. That was bad enough. But the worst part of all would soon follow. Hollywood would pay Kiki a visit, while Lacey's chances of getting discovered were ruined. Lacey wished Kiki would just disappear for a while so she could be the Queen. That's the way it was supposed to be.

"Hey, Lacey! What's happening?" a voice shouted from a car waiting at the traffic light in front of the green. "Long time."

"Why don't all those geeks lay off me," Lacey muttered, not bothering to look up.

"Some geek. Who's that cutie pie?" Renée whispered to Lacey.

Lacey looked up to see an extremely handsome guy in a black BMW convertible. "Junior?" she called out.

"Hi, Lacey. I go by Lars now," Vaughn's brother said. He flashed Lacey an irresistible grin.

Lacey got up and went over to the car. "Wow, I hardly recognized you." She'd known Junior Cutter all her life, but never once had she even considered him to be anything more than dullsville. Especially compared to Vaughn. Now she marveled at his flashy new look, his white smile against his deep tan, and his longish wavy brown hair. He was sporting a pair of hundred-dollar Ray-bans and a tiny gold earring in one pierced ear. Wow! It was more than just his name. College really seemed to have brought him out of his shell. He was definitely cute, and a lot more friendly than his *little* brother.

Lacey rested her arm on his door. "Looks like you scored some nice wheels!" she said.

"Birthday present from Father. I'm twenty-one now." Junior grinned. "Legal and free!"

"Lucky you," Lacey said. She couldn't get over how different he seemed. "What are you doing home, Junior—I mean, Lars?"

"I'm going to be working for the old man this summer. Doing that executive thing," he said proudly. "How about you, Lacey?" He paused. "You're looking as good as ever. Seems like good ol' Paradiso's been treating you well."

"Aren't you sweet," Lacey said. How little this boy knows about me and this damn town, Lacey thought. But it's just as well.

A horn tooted behind Junior. Lacey noticed that there were a half dozen cars waiting behind him. "Better be going, Lacey. I'll give you a call," he shouted out as he drove away.

You do that, Lacey thought as she went back to where Renée was sitting. "Lars Cutter, Junior!" she said. "Wonder of wonders."

"You know, that light changed twice while you guys were flirting. Better watch out, Lacey. He is *into* you."

"He's the one who better watch out," Lacey said with a grin. "How'd he get so sexy?"

"I don't know, but I wish there were a few more around like him," Renée said.

"Stick with Doug, Renée. You guys are meant for each other. You're better off leaving the Cutter family to me."

"Looks like you'd stand a better chance with Junior in your dad's jet, than with V—" Renée quickly covered her mouth with her hand.

Lacey felt the hairs on the back of her neck stand up. "Who told you about my date with Vaughn?" she demanded.

"I'm sorry, Lacey. I didn't mean that. It just slipped out."

"Who told you that pack of lies?" Lacey pressed.

"It's a small town, Lace. I heard it from my brother. I guess Vaughn told him at wrestling practice."

Anger and annoyance, and something else . . . shame? . . . flashed through Lacey. "Well, I promise you, Renée, it didn't go the way you heard.

Vaughn wouldn't be advertising the real version of that night for the world."

"So what *did* happen?" Renée asked.

"Let's just say that things didn't work out the way he expected. Vaughn wanted a lot more from me than I was interested in giving," Lacey said, crossing her fingers behind her back.

"But he wasn't really the one who gave you the black eye, was he?" Renée asked.

Lacey gulped. Could she tell the truth to Renée? Renée had come a long way since her brief stay in an institution. Maybe she could handle things better because she had confronted her problems. But Lacey wasn't ready to let the world know about her father. She couldn't. "I just fell. That's all. But Vaughn deserved to take the blame. Believe me, after the way he treated me the other night, he deserved a lot more than that."

"Sure, Lacey. I believe you," Renée said. "Really." But Lacey thought she sounded leery. "Well, it's practically all healed. You can barely see it."

Lacey frowned. She thought she'd managed to keep Friday night a secret. With everything else going on in Paradiso, she had figured the botched date in the jet wouldn't get too much airtime among the local gossips. But if Renée knew, who else had heard?

Oh, no! Penny! Lacey thought, an alarm going off in her head. She'll drive me crazy if she finds out.

66

"How about Penny?" Lacey was almost afraid to ask. "Does she know about my date with Vaughn?"

Renée shrugged. "Never mentioned it. Why?"

"Because we were supposed to hang out that night and I canceled on her. I sort of lied to her so that Vaughn and I could go out. What a mistake that was. Anyway, you're sure she doesn't know?" Lacey asked, studying Renée's reaction.

"Pretty sure." Renée shook her head. "No, she doesn't know. She'd have mentioned it. She'd definitely have said something."

"Renée," Lacey ordered, "whatever you do, *don't* tell her. You know how she gets if I pay the slightest bit of attention to anyone besides her. She'd take it too hard."

"I understand, Lacey," Renée said. "Yeah, she really idolizes you. But I think you're safe on that score. She can't stop talking about how great her date with Hal was on Friday. She was raving about the food you had sent over to them. She said you made her weekend great."

The Pinkertons' gourmet chef had prepared a special feast for Penny and Hal. Lacey's plan to gain Penny's forgiveness had worked like a charm. "And I wasn't even with her. I guess I mean a lot to Penny," Lacey said, smiling. "I'd hate our friendship to get messed up because of one little lie."

"Well, if I were you, Lacey, I wouldn't worry about it. You're definitely Penny's all-time hero."

Lacey was relieved. "Maybe I'll head over to Bolton's and visit her at work. I'll get her to convince her dad to let her out early so I can buy her an ice cream. How many nuts and bolts can that girl sell in one day, anyway?"

"Or wrenches and ropes," Renée added. "I was thinking how Penny could have been the one to sell the murder weapon to Spike. Creepy, huh?"

"I suppose," Lacey said, getting up to go. "You want to come along? I'm buying for everyone."

"No, I think I'll go check up on Doug. He said he was studying for finals in the library. I'll see if I can help him flunk out. That'll keep him here another year." Renée laughed, giving Lacey a hug. "Give Pen a big kiss for me. Hey, you know, Lacey, maybe you need someone like Junior to lift your spirits. Why wait for his call?"

"Something tells me I won't have to wait too long for Junior. I'll see you, babe," she said, heading for the hardware store.

But deep down the Peach Blossom contest *was* making her miserable. The contest was fixed. I know it. I should have won, she said to herself. The idea of spending the next week and a half as Kiki's lady-in-waiting was a total nightmare. She couldn't reverse the decision. Not even Daddy had that kind of power. But what if she could make Kiki resign? Like she had originally intended to do. If Kiki, on her own accord, decided to back down, then the committee would have to make Lacey the winner. And she'd know the whole routine already.

The rehearsals! That's it. What if tomorrow's rehearsal went a little differently than planned? Lacey grinned to herself. Maybe a little scare was all it would take for Queen Kiki to abdicate her throne.

CHAPTER 9

Raven made her way up Winding Hill Road. The spacious houses and the rolling green lawns were bathed in the golden afternoon light. It seemed as if everything was perfect in this part of Paradiso. But you couldn't judge it by its storybook cover.

Raven thought about the Pinkertons, way up at the top of the hill in their modern castle. April's murder and the fight over the mall had brought their problems right out into the open. That and the very prominent black eye Lacey had gotten the week before. Everyone was whispering that her father had given it to her. And that both Lacey's parents drank like fish.

The Cutters had managed to keep their problems quieter, but Raven knew that a lot went on behind the walls of the tranquil, proper New England–style estate. Mr. Cutter exercised complete control over his two sons. Junior was the perfect double for his father in every way—a budding business tycoon. Vaughn, on the other hand, resisted. But when he resisted too much, his father retaliated by threatening to cut him out of the family.

Raven walked by Kiki's house. Maybe the De Santises were one of the few families who really did live happily ever after. Kiki's parents seemed genuinely nice and in love with each other. And Kiki was the Peach Blossom Queen of Paradiso.

Raven hated the shiver of envy that she felt for her friend. But Kiki's parents could afford to send her to any college in the country. Raven needed that scholarship money more than either of the other girls in the contest.

But scholarship or no scholarship, Raven had made a decision. She opened the small pocketbook she had bought at Regina's Antiques in Sacramento. It was an old, fifties-style bag of black patent leather that went perfectly with the full pony-skirted dress Raven wore. The bag opened easily, since the clasp didn't work too well. Inside, Raven could see the roll of green bills Calvin Pinkerton had given to her, secured with a rubber band. The roll was short two hundred dollars —the money that Raven had used to pay the doctor. But what was Mr. Pinkerton going to do? Take her to court over it? Just let him admit in public that he'd resorted to bribery to build his mall.

Worries about Mama and about college had kept Raven up all night. But she just couldn't allow Calvin

Pinkerton to buy her this way. She thought of Papa's broken pride. And her own. She couldn't take the money.

Raven quickened her pace as she got to the high stone wall around the Cutter estate. She passed the house and continued up the hill. She heard a car coming up the road and glanced behind her.

Oh, no! Vaughn's Jaguar! She started to run. She could hear the car get nearer. How could she explain her presence here to Vaughn? She pumped her legs. *Faster!*

But she wasn't quick enough. She heard Vaughn honking his horn to get her attention. Without slowing down, she glanced over her shoulder. Vaughn had passed his driveway and was coming up the hill. Raven looked for a place to duck. But what good was it? She'd been spotted already. She slowed to a walk as Vaughn pulled up next to her and put on the emergency brake.

"Hi," he said, trying out a tentative-looking smile on her.

Normally Vaughn's smile did funny things to Raven. Right now, though, she was too busy trying to come up with what she was going to tell him to let him work his charms on her. "Hi," she answered nervously.

Vaughn asked the inevitable. "Any special reason for coming into my neck of the woods?" He looked as handsome as ever, his chiseled features lightly tanned, his wavy brown hair streaked by the sun.

"Um, I came to visit Kiki," Raven lied. "I wanted to congratulate her again."

She could tell Vaughn didn't believe her. "Is that why you went right by the De Santises' house? Besides, Kiki's not home. I saw her driving down Old Town Road with Hope Hubbard a little while ago." Vaughn's smile faded to an expression of uncertainty.

Hope and Kiki? Raven hadn't realized they were such good friends. But now that Kiki was out from under Lacey's shadow, she had more of a chance to hang out with other people. Better people, Raven thought. "I, um, I know Kiki's not home. I stopped off there, and when I didn't find her, I—I thought I'd take a walk," she lied to Vaughn.

"Up Winding Hill Road?" A note of bitterness crept into Vaughn's voice. "Where all us spoiled rich kids live?"

Raven felt herself turning red. She'd said some pretty harsh things to Vaughn when they'd had their big fight. She shrugged her shoulders. As she did, she felt her handbag slip down her arm.

She made a dive for the bag, but it hit the ground before she could catch it. She watched in horror as the contents of the bag spilled out onto the street. Her keys, her change purse, a tube of lipstick—and Calvin Pinkerton's money! Raven gasped as the roll of bills disappeared beneath one of the Jaguar's front

73

tires. She raced over and stuck her hand under the car, groping blindly for the money.

Vaughn got out of the car. As Raven searched frantically for the money, he picked up her pocketbook and some of the other things that had spilled out of it. Then he reached under the car with her. "What are you looking for?"

"No, Vaughn!" she exclaimed sharply. "I'll get it!" But it was too late. His reach was longer, and he came out with Calvin Pinkerton's money.

Raven's breath caught. She reached for the roll of bills. Vaughn closed his hand around both her hand and the money. "Let go, Vaughn. Give it to me," she demanded.

He held on with his wrestler's grip. "Not until you tell me what you're doing with all this money," Vaughn said. "And don't tell me that you had a good day at the café."

Raven shook her arm in desperation, trying to break free of Vaughn. But he was too strong. She stopped fighting. She felt the money locked between their palms, Vaughn's warm hand around hers. She looked up at him. Their eyes met. She felt a rush of the old electricity.

Vaughn must have too. "Tell me," he said more gently. "You can trust me."

Raven didn't know what to do. "Vaughn, you've got to give it back to me. It's not mine."

"Oh, it's not?" Vaughn arched an eyebrow. "And

74

don't tell me you've become a bank robber in the last week either."

Raven felt flushed. "Look, I'm returning it to the person it belongs to. It got—lost."

Vaughn held on to her—and the money. "Oh." He looked up Winding Hill Road in the direction Raven had been running in. Then he looked back at her. His expression darkened. "Oh," he said again, with more understanding this time. And then, "My God, Raven, is that why you left SCAM?" He pulled his hand away from her as if she had a contagious disease. "At least I was honest about why I quit!" he said.

Raven closed her hand around Cal Pinkerton's money. Vaughn shoved her pocketbook at her, and she took it, stuffing the bills inside. "Vaughn, you don't understand," she protested. She tried to keep herself under control, but her voice cracked. "Mama's so sick. She could die. And there's no insurance to pay her medical bills."

Vaughn's face softened. "I know, Raven. And I'm really sorry. But don't you see? You quit SCAM for your family—just what you got so mad at me for doing. And you took that money on top of everything."

"Vaughn, I'm returning the money," Raven said.

"And the lies you told the other members of SCAM? Don't they deserve to know the truth?"

Raven blinked hard. She didn't want to cry in

front of Vaughn. "They weren't lies. Everything I told them was true. I just left out one of the reasons why I had to quit."

"The main reason. The real reason." Raven could hear the anger building in Vaughn's voice, and it scared her. She had seen him explode when he got mad like this.

Suddenly Raven wondered why she was letting Vaughn make her feel so ashamed. "Well, at least I'm trying to correct my mistakes," she said. "What are you doing? Driving around in that car your parents paid for and spending their money."

She was sorry as soon as the words were out of her mouth. It was as if Vaughn's temper were catching. Raven knew that deep down it was out of frustration. She was angry at Vaughn, but he still made her heart race. It was hard to be this close to him and not want to be with him. He hadn't been far from her thoughts for a moment since their fight.

"Look, Vaughn, I didn't mean that," Raven apologized.

Vaughn held her gaze for a moment. "I don't know, Raven. I think you did. You know, you get mad at people for treating you like you're from the wrong side of the tracks? Well, you treat me the same way."

Raven clicked her tongue. "Vaughn, I said I was sorry."

Vaughn sighed, and Raven could see all the fight going out of him. "Well, I'm sorry too. We keep on ending up on the same subject—me and my family with all our piles of money, and you and your family without it. I was wrong to think that it didn't matter."

Raven felt a flicker of annoyance. "I don't think it's that simple. Vaughn, you just don't understand the kind of pressure I've been under lately."

"Welcome to the club," Vaughn replied. He stared at her, as if trying to decide what to do next. Suddenly he shook his head and climbed into the Jag. He gave the door a slam. "You don't have to be poor to have problems. See you, Raven." He pulled a U-turn, his tires squealing, and took off back down the road.

Raven felt the knot in her throat swelling, and a prickling behind her eyes, but she refused to cry. Not for Vaughn, not now at least. She marched up Winding Hill Road toward the Pinkerton mansion, to tell Lacey's father that he could keep his dirty money.

CHAPTER 10

Kiki dropped Hope off at her house and headed straight for the sheriff's station. She was sure that Spike's hammer and wrench would shed new light on his case. She climbed out of the Trooper, holding her shoulder bag with his tools close to her. She felt a rush of happiness thinking that her wish about Spike was about to come true.

Kiki pushed open the door to the station. The sheriff would listen to her. After all, I am the Queen, and my royal word won't be ignored. She giggled to herself.

"Hello, Miss De Santis," Sheriff Rodriguez said from behind his desk. "Nice to see you again. I hope you brought him news about his brothers." He nodded toward the hall that led to Spike's cell. "That's all he's been asking about."

Spike was waiting for her! Kiki felt her heart skip. Spike's dark good looks and deep, quiet inner fire had been on her mind all day. She couldn't wait to tell him about the tools and see his spirit lifted. Maybe he'd even agree to change his mind about his guilty plea. Then Sheriff Rodriguez would have to do something.

Kiki rushed down the dimly lit hallway. She found Spike standing in front of his cell window, looking out at some kids playing on their bicycles behind the police station. Seeing how his broad, muscular shoulders were sagging under his prison jumpsuit, Kiki felt a pang.

"Spike," Kiki said softly.

"Look how much fun they're having. They're playing cops and robbers." He turned around and faced Kiki. He looked so tired, so worried. "You visited my brothers, didn't you? How are they?" She saw the shadowed crescents below his intense brown eyes, and her heart ached for him.

"They're fine, Spike," Kiki said. "They miss you an awful lot."

Spike nodded gravely. But Kiki could see the anger and the bitterness behind his vague smile. It just wasn't fair. Here he was, spending all his time alone in a dingy cell where he certainly didn't belong, and the real killer was roaming around free. "How are you doing, Spike?" Kiki asked softly.

"Me?" Spike gave a short, hard laugh. His fists clenched and unclenched at his sides. "Not bad for a caged bird. But let's not talk about me, Kiki." He looked at her for a silent moment. Kiki felt his gaze on her—a touch without touching. She smiled shyly. "How about you?" Spike finally said. "You look happy."

"I am. It's been a great day. Until now, that is." Kiki couldn't take her eyes off Spike. She studied his dark, deep-set eyes, his full mouth, the line of his nose.

Kiki moved closer to him. "You ready to change your plea yet? It would make your little brothers real happy to have you come home."

Spike shook his head. "I'd still lose. Kiki, it's sweet of you to come, but don't try to talk me into fighting again. Like I said yesterday, I've lost already."

There was a moment of tense silence. Spike turned away from Kiki and took another look outside his window. "You just don't understand, Kiki. It's me against the world. I can't fight it."

"Spike," Kiki spoke softly. "I think I have something that will change your mind." She reached into her bag and pulled out his hammer and wrench. "Look what I brought."

Spike's eyes opened wide. "Are you crazy? What, are you going to spring me loose? Man, you've really flipped!"

Kiki let out a nervous laugh. "You don't understand, Spike. Look." She held up the tools for him to see. " 'C. N.' You see here? And here," she said, pointing to the etched letters on the shaft of the

80

wrench. " 'Carlos Navarrone.' Now *this* wrench is definitely yours. Unlike the murder weapon, which wasn't marked at all. Hope and I found these in your trailer. Your brothers were trying to fix one of their bikes."

Spike came up to the front of the cell and clasped his hands around the metal bars. "Kiki, I already told the federal agents that the wrench wasn't mine. They didn't believe me. They just looked at me and said, 'Sure, kid, that's what they all say.' No, Kiki. Case closed. Closed!" Spike insisted, his grip tightening around the bars.

"But what about the engraving? Did you tell them about that, too?" Kiki asked, frightened.

He shook his head. "No. But . . ."

"Well, I'm going to show these tools to Sheriff Rodriguez. He'll understand." But Kiki saw only more doubt in Spike's eyes. "Spike, what's wrong? He's known you since you were a kid. He never thought you were guilty, either. Not until you confessed. Now he has to listen."

But Kiki could see the tension racing through Spike's body. Despair tightened his face. He shook the bars, as if brute strength alone could free him.

Kiki reached out and wrapped her hands around his, stilling him. His hands were warm. The electricity was instant. "Spike, I'm frightened for you." She looked into his dark eyes. "I was daydreaming about the Peach Blossom Festival. You were there, Spike,

81

having the most fun of anybody. Because you were free."

Kiki could feel Spike start to pull away. But she held on tightly. "It sounds like a great dream," he said. "But that's all it was, I'm afraid. A dream."

"But what if it could happen? What if you could be there, celebrating with the rest of us?"

Spike smiled sadly. "I'd like that. I'd like to see how happy you'll be that day. And how beautiful you'll look."

Kiki felt dizzy with the strangest mixture of sorrow and joy. She was overpowered with an impulsive urge. She leaned forward and gave Spike a light, tender kiss on the lips. Pressed up against the metal bars, Spike kissed back. Kiki could feel his moist lips trembling.

Kiki's heart fluttered. She pulled back and looked up at him. "Spike, will you be my date for the Festival Ball?"

"Kiki . . ."

"Please don't say no, Spike. I want my dream to come true. And I want for these bars not to be here anymore."

Spike started to shake his head.

"Don't let me down, Spike," Kiki implored, her throat tightening, her words becoming choked. "And don't let yourself down. Your life is too important. If you can, will you take me? Will you take the Queen to the ball?"

Kiki noticed a tear forming in Spike's eye. He nodded. "I'd love to go with you, Kiki. It would be an honor, Your Majesty."

They looked at each other for a long moment. "Then I have some work to do."

She backed up to the doorway, holding his gaze until she turned the corner and his cell disappeared from view.

Sheriff Rodriguez was staring out the front window, his feet propped up on his desk. "Everything I've read about you is true, Kiki. It's very kind of you to come visit Carlos."

"I just want people to know the truth. Spike's innocent, sir."

"I was afraid you were going to say that." He pulled his feet off his desk and swiveled around to face her. The sheriff wore a pained look. "It's still hard for me to believe. But, Kiki, I have his official confession. Signed and witnessed."

Kiki reached into her bag and put the tools down on the sheriff's desk. "These are from Spike's house. All Spike's tools are hand engraved with his name. Even the tiny little ones," she said confidently.

"Hmmm. 'Carlos Navarrone,'" the sheriff mumbled as he examined them.

"You see? He's innocent," Kiki said.

The sheriff gave Kiki a sad, sympathetic smile. "I wish it were that simple. First of all, I doubt that Spike would have committed the crime in question using a weapon that bore his name. Maybe it was a

83

new tool that he hadn't engraved yet. I don't know. The fact that the murder weapon was found at Spike and April's secret meeting place makes for a very bad case against him. And his hiding from us for so long —well, that makes it much worse. I'm not sure Spike meant to kill April Lovewell, but all signs still point to him, Kiki." He shook his head. "I'm sorry, but there's just not enough evidence to the contrary. The federal agents have years of experience, and I'm just a small-town sheriff. No, this wouldn't change their minds."

"But Spike said he was forced into a confession. Don't you see—he's being framed," Kiki's voice rose in protest.

"It's possible, of course. But framed by who?" The sheriff took the tools and put them in his top drawer. "I'm going to hold on to these, Kiki, just in case. But between you and me, I'm afraid Spike is not going to get off unless the someone else is caught. Red-handed."

Kiki felt a stab of fear. "That would mean he'd have to strike again."

Sheriff Rodriguez raised his eyebrows. "Yes, that's right. That's exactly what he'd have to do." He gave Kiki a concerned look. "Be careful, Kiki, please. Don't go looking for trouble."

Kiki froze. If she was right, trouble would come looking for her. One Queen was already dead. Would Kiki be next?

CHAPTER 11

Calvin Pinkerton's golf club glimmered dangerously in the strong sunlight as he pulled it back behind him. In one swift move he swung. A hollow crack split the air. Raven watched the ball sail through the sky in a perfect arc. It came down deep in the endless stretch of lush lawn behind the Pinkerton Estates.

Mr. Pinkerton positioned another ball on the tee. Ready, swing—*thud*. The club hit the ball at an off angle. It gave only a few feeble jumps before rolling to a stop well within sight. Mr. Pinkerton gave a fierce scowl and hurled the driver after the ball, like a spear. Clearly Calvin Pinkerton did not take it mildly when something didn't go his way. He stormed after the club and grabbed it from the ground. As he turned to walk back to the tee, he caught sight of Raven.

Suddenly he was all smiles. "Well, look who we

have here! Our Stanford scholar." He was wearing white linen slacks and a blue Izod shirt. His hair was combed perfectly in place. He looked like a walking, talking ad for GQ—right down to his tropical tan, gold Rolex, and capped white teeth.

Raven flinched at his sugarcoated greeting. "Hello, Mr. Pinkerton," she said evenly.

Calvin Pinkerton set up another tee. "What can I do for you?" he asked, addressing the ball. He swung his club and hit his mark square on. The ball went flying high into the cloudless sky.

Raven dug into her pocketbook. Her heart was racing. Her fingers found the roll of bills. "I changed my mind. I don't want this." She thrust the money toward him.

Calvin Pinkerton turned toward her, a scowl forming on his tanned, even-featured face. "But I thought we'd come to a rather nice little understanding."

"Mr. Pinkerton, I made a mistake the other day. I was weak," she confessed, wincing inside. "But now I know what I did was wrong. I let a lot of people down. Most of all, myself."

His eyes lit with cold fury. "Am I hearing you right?" he asked, all the cloying sweetness gone from his voice.

Raven stood with her hand out. "I can't take your money. And I won't give up my fight for the scrublands." She paused, glancing down at the wad of bills. "It's all there . . . minus two hundred. But I promise you I'll pay it back. Every penny."

Mr. Pinkerton didn't make a move for the money. He stood, swinging his club back and forth slowly, like a pendulum. "You're making a big mistake, little lady," he said darkly. "Are you quite sure?"

Raven nodded. She looked out over the green field dotted with stately trees. "Think how it would be if someone put up a mall right here and took all this away." She gestured at his lawn with the roll of bills.

Calvin Pinkerton let out a raw laugh. "I don't think so, my dear." He addressed her as if he had just tasted something sour. "No, no one's going to build the mall here. Not on my turf." He tapped his golf club against the ground for emphasis, as if to say "Mine, all mine." He shook his head. "We're not going to build it here because we're going to build it in *your* backyard. Though I do regret the disturbance it will cause to your poor, sick mother. By the way, how is Rosa?"

Raven gritted her teeth. What a low blow, to bring her mother into this. Calvin Pinkerton was truly a slime. "I'll manage to take care of Mama—without your help," she said angrily.

"You know, I thought you were a smart young woman," Mr. Pinkerton said. "Don't you know you'll never be able to beat me? What can you do against all my money and power?"

87

"Maybe I won't win," Raven said. "But at least I'll know I did what I could. Honestly."

"Don't be a fool!" Calvin Pinkerton snarled, and slammed the club into the grass. "When the Greenway Mall is finished, you'll have absolutely nothing. If you keep to our deal, you'll have a college education and your mother's health."

For a brief moment Raven almost felt sorry for Lacey, the princess locked away in the castle with the evil king. "Are you going to take this, or should I put it on the ground?" Raven asked, shaking the bundle of bills.

Calvin Pinkerton lunged forward and grabbed the money out of Raven's hand. "Watch out for yourself, Miss Raven Cruz," he threatened, pointing at her with the head of his golf club. "You won't like having me as your enemy again."

The club hovered in the sunlight, heavy and blunt and deadly. But Raven wasn't going to let Mr. Pinkerton frighten her. Not again. She turned and walked away, slowly and deliberately. She was free.

CHAPTER 12

Hope and Jess were locked in a passionate kiss when they were interrupted by someone banging on the door of Gardner's Auto Body and Repair.

"Just ignore it," Jess murmured, his lips brushing her neck as he spoke.

"Ignore what?" Hope giggled. She drew Jess back into her embrace. Looking into his cornflower blue eyes, she still couldn't believe that Jess was her boyfriend. His sweet face and lean swimmer's physique were a deadly combination Hope couldn't resist. His lips were so warm and soft on hers. She ran her fingers through his thick, wavy blond hair, breathing in the spicy warmth of his skin. Jess ran his hands lightly up and down her back.

But the knocking continued.

"We're closed!" Jess yelled out. Then he whispered in Hope's ear, "Can't they read the sign?" He kissed the side of her face.

She didn't want him to stop.

"Jess! It's me! Vaughn!" came the voice from the other side of the door.

Jess let go of Hope. "Oh." He looked at Hope and rolled his eyes. "Some timing, huh?" he whispered.

Hope nodded, stifling a laugh.

Jess flicked on the lights as he made his way to the door. Hope blinked in the brightness, suddenly feeling a bit shy. She was sitting on an old bench seat that had been removed from a car; the upholstery was worn, the stuffing coming out in places. Around her there were several cars in various stages of repair and a shop scattered with tools. Every one of them marked, according to Jess.

Hope ran her fingers through her hair, trying to make herself look presentable, as Jess opened the door of the shop to let Vaughn in. Hope saw he was carrying a very full duffel bag.

"Hey, man, what's happening?" Jess said, clasping Vaughn's shoulder. "You look like you're going on a trip."

"You could say that," Vaughn said somberly, flicking away a sun-streaked lock of hair that had fallen over his forehead. He caught sight of Hope. "Hi, Hope. Listen, I'm sorry if I barged in on you guys." He set his bag down on the floor. "But I needed a place to go."

"Another fight with your parents?" Jess asked.

Vaughn shook his head. "I didn't see any point to a

repeat performance. All they'd do is tell me who I can spend time with and what I'm supposed to think. I've heard it before. So . . . I'm moving out."

"Just like that?" Hope asked. "Where are you going to live?" She tried to imagine packing her bags and leaving the small, neat house where she'd grown up. Next year she'd be going off to college on the East Coast, but she'd still have her room to come back to on vacations. Mom would still be there for her. The tiny house she'd lived in all her life would still be home. Sure, she'd had her troubles with Mom, especially over the feud with April's parents, but she couldn't imagine leaving home like Vaughn was doing—and never coming back.

Vaughn shrugged. "I guess I'm going to have to start looking for a job and a place to rent. Jess, I wondered if it would be okay if I stayed with you and your father for a few days. Just until I figure things out."

"I'll have to ask Dad," Jess said, "but I'm sure he'll say it's fine. Wow, that's pretty heavy," he added.

"Yeah, it is." Vaughn sat down on top of his overnight bag. "Maybe it seems spoiled, but I've never had to think about getting work before. I've got a few bonds from Granddad, but I guess I'm going to have to write to Dartmouth and tell them that I won't be coming in September. That was Dad's idea anyway. His good old alma mater."

"But it's a good school," Hope commented. She

had considered applying there herself, before she'd been accepted early admission at MIT.

"It's an expensive school," Vaughn said. He let out a short laugh. "Maybe *I* should have entered the contest for Peach Blossom Queen."

"About time Paradiso got hip to equality of the sexes," Jess remarked.

Hope laughed. "Boy, Lacey would have been even more furious than she already is if she'd lost to you, Vaughn."

Vaughan's mouth curled in a lopsided grin. "Man, it would be a pleasure to beat her out of the crown after all those lies she told Willa Flicker."

"Just 'cause you wouldn't get romantic with her, huh?" Jess said.

"Yeah, and the worst part is, I almost fell for her little seduction scene." He shook his head as if in disbelief that anyone could be so dumb. "I'm an easy mark for a pretty face. I mean, I should never have agreed to another date with her. There was a reason I broke up with Lacey in the first place."

Jess laughed. "Don't take it so hard, man. You're not the only one who got put under her evil spell. Forgive me, Hope," he added.

Hope laughed along, but she did feel a little jealous of Lacey. She hadn't been with Jess long enough to feel totally secure. And Lacey *was* gorgeous, even if she was hard to take. "It's history, right?" she said uneasily. Jess and Vaughn were both on the long list of Lacey's ex-boyfriends.

"You know it," Jess assured her. He came back over and sat down with her on the old car seat, putting an arm around her shoulder. Hope snuggled up to him, shyly but happily.

"I should have known better too," Vaughn said sheepishly. "I don't know. I think it was her offer to let me fly her dad's jet that really did it. And I have to admit, it was flattering to have her paying all that attention to me after Raven and I had that huge fight." Vaughn's voice filled with misery. Hope could tell how much he missed her, just by the way he said her name. He shook his head. "You know, things are supposed to be so great around here, now that the murder's solved. . . ."

Hope looked at Jess. "Maybe we should tell him," she said.

"Tell me what?" Vaughn asked.

"I don't know if it is solved," Hope said slowly. "I was explaining it all to Jess a little while earlier."

Vaughn raised an eyebrow. "Hope, Spike confessed. Everyone knows that."

Hope sighed. "Vaughn, it's more complicated than you think." She filled him in on Kiki's visit to the jail, and on what she had discovered out at the trailer.

Vaughn whistled. "Wow! That's pretty wild. I mean, why would that one wrench you guys found not have Spike's name on it?" Vaughn frowned. "Unless he bought it to use on April. Then he wouldn't exactly have wanted anyone to know whose it was."

Jess shook his head. "Don't you think if he'd planned it all out he would have used something else? A wrench doesn't seem like the best weapon you could come up with to commit a murder. And if it wasn't planned beforehand, he'd have used whatever he had on him. Which would have been something with his name on it. Someone else came down to that tree to kill April."

As she listened to Jess and Vaughn, Hope felt an overpowering uneasiness. In her mind's eye, April stood under the tall tree. A faceless figure snuck up behind her, brandishing a sharply gleaming monkey wrench. Hope brought her hands to her stomach, nauseated. "Guys, you're talking about my cousin."

"Oh, jeez, Hope, I'm sorry," Jess said. "I know how much you loved April. I'm not forgetting about her. But I guess it's easier to try to be all hard-nosed, trying to figure things out, than to think about the part where someone I knew was the victim of something so horrible. I'm sorry," Jess repeated.

Hope could feel herself trembling in Jess's arms. "It's okay. I can really understand what you're saying. I've been doing the same thing."

"I know you have," Jess said gingerly. "Maybe that's the problem. Maybe all your sleuthing to find out who did it and why is a way of avoiding going back to your regular life—and having to accept that April's not a part of it anymore."

"Maybe Spike really is guilty," Vaughn added.

Hope broke away from Jess's hug. "So you guys really believe Spike Navarrone did it?" she demanded.

Silence filled the garage. Jess finally shook his head. "I always thought Spike was a good guy. Quiet, kept to himself. We used to talk about fixing up cars and bikes and stuff sometimes, and then he'd get really psyched up. I don't know. He seemed sort of gentle under all the biker stuff. You know?"

"That's what Kiki thinks too," Hope said.

"Sounds like Kiki has kind of a thing going for Spike," Vaughn commented. "You know, one time when she and my brother and I were having this kind of truth-or-dare session over at her pool, she said she thought he was cute."

Hope sighed. "Yeah, I think she likes Spike," Hope admitted. "But, Vaughn, maybe she's right about him. There's still the whole business about the wrench not being marked. And don't forget. They might know it's the murder weapon, but it didn't have Spike's fingerprints on it."

"But it was under that tree," Vaughn said. "Their tree. Maybe Spike wore gloves. Motorcycle gloves."

"I don't know," Hope said. "There's something about it that just doesn't jibe. Why would a murderer kill someone under a tree with their initials right on it, for pete's sake? It just doesn't make sense." The more Hope thought about it, the more she was convinced. But how could she prove it?

Vaughn raised his shoulders. "Okay. Then if Spike didn't do it, who did?"

"Well, there was that article Willa Flicker wrote about the Pinkerton Connection," Hope ventured.

" 'Murder for a Mall.' Isn't that what she called it?" Jess asked.

"Right," Vaughn said. "She hinted that Lacey was involved." He shook his head. "I don't know. As much as I think she deserves for me to belt her one, I can't see her as a murderer. A spoiled brat, now that's another story."

"Vaughn, she does have the same size footprint as the murderer," Hope said. She shuddered, the faceless killer replaced by a picture of Lacey, holding a wrench and grinning evilly.

Vaughn frowned. "Hope, I know Lacey's not your favorite person," he said. "And I can understand, but still . . ."

Hope felt a breath of annoyance. Did Vaughn think she was suspicious of Lacey just because she was jealous? "It's not like that," she said. "We all know Lacey, and if she wanted the crown enough . . ."

"Or if someone else wanted her to win badly enough . . ." Jess suggested.

Vaughn's face darkened. "Raven told me that Mrs. Pinkerton threatened Kiki that she should drop out of the contest. Is that what you mean? Wow. Kiki could be in danger!"

Hope felt cold. Was Kiki next on the murderer's list, now that she'd been chosen Peggy Sue?

"Darla Pinkerton probably wasn't the only one who wanted April out of the way," Jess said.

"You mean maybe one of the other Pinks did it for Lacey?" Hope said. "Yeah, I've thought about that." In fact, two names were already in Hope's computer file of clues. "Remember how we saw Renée Henderson in that blue-hooded sweatshirt that looked like the one whoever chased me was wearing?" she said. "And then there's Penny. You know how she's always sticking up for Lacey and worshiping the ground she walks on. Besides, she was the one who told me about Spike and April's secret spot. What if she didn't find it accidentally, but she knows about it because she followed April?"

"Or what if Willa Flicker's behind it because all the stories are good for her career?" Jess said.

"It's possible," Hope answered. "But if I had to bet on it, I still think Lacey's the one."

"So now we're back to square one," Vaughn said. "Who killed Peggy Sue? Are we really sure Spike didn't?"

Hope shook her head. "I'm sure. And it feels awful knowing that he's going to pay for someone else's crime." She looked at the metal toolbox near one of the cars that was being worked on. Even that had the

97

words "Gardner's Auto" stamped on the lid. Spike's tools had been more crudely marked—with his name scratched in by hand with something sharp. But they'd been marked just the same. The hideous wrench Hope had found under the tree had nothing written on it.

Nothing except murder.

CHAPTER 13

Kiki twisted the dial on her locker left and right, back and forth. Hopeless. She simply couldn't get the combination right. She couldn't remember this ever happening before. But given the circumstances, it wasn't hard to understand. She'd been on emotional overload all day long. She just couldn't think straight.

From the minute she walked into school this morning, kids had been coming up to her and giving her a pat on the back or wishing "her highness" a royally good day. Kiki would feel the rush of being Queen, then she'd think about Spike sitting in jail. And she'd get sad—and scared. The real killer was still out there. She'd find herself scrutinizing each and every one who congratulated her, trying to decide whether that person could be the real killer. No one was above suspicion.

She'd even given a second thought to Winston Purdy III. It was the way he had said that he'd bet all along that Kiki would win the contest. *Bet?* Kiki had thought. How much had that bet been worth to him? Enough to have killed April?

"Hey, Kiki, having fun?" Janice Campbell said as she raced down the hall. "When are we going to celebrate?"

Kiki waved to Janice as she hurried off. "Soon, Janice. Promise." Oh my God, Janice, Kiki thought. She finished in fourth place in the Peach Blossom balloting. What if she had . . .

Kiki shook her head. No, don't be crazy. It's not Janice. And it's certainly not Winston.

Only three things were certain. One, Kiki was sure Spike was innocent. Two, she didn't know who the real killer was. And three, she still couldn't remember her combination. She tried a few more numbers. But the only ones that stuck in her mind were 35–23–35, the famous combination—Hope's locker where April was found. Everybody at school knew it because the numbers supposedly matched Lacey's measurements.

Kiki felt a hand rest on her shoulder. She let out a frightened gasp as she turned around. Bobby Deeter stood there smiling at her, his eager brown eyes gazing at her from behind wirerimmed glasses. "Bobby, my God, you scared me half to death," she said, catching her breath.

"Then fall into my arms and I'll put your fears to rest," he said, opening them up for her to follow his lead.

But Kiki backed up against her locker. She could see the hurt in Bobby's eyes. Poor Bobby. "I . . . I . . . I'm late for my rehearsal, Bobby. I should have been there ten minutes ago. I know it's silly, but for some reason I just couldn't remember my combination," she said with a shrug. She hoped she could lighten the mood a little, but it didn't work. Any girl would be lucky to have Bobby. He was the editor of the *Bell* and captain of the Debating Team. His schoolboy grin and sad brown eyes were irresistible. Or they had been once, Kiki thought.

"Ten, fourteen, twelve," Bobby said, looking down at his feet. "The day of the big Paradiso–Melrose play-off, midnight. Our first kiss. Somehow I'm not surprised you forgot." He shrugged. "Here, let me get it."

Kiki watched Bobby as he opened up the locker. He wouldn't even look at her. Had she hurt him that much? "I'm sorry, Bobby. You know I've never been great with numbers."

"That must explain why you haven't called me lately. I guess you've forgotten my phone number too."

Go ahead, Bobby. Don't stop now. What else have I done lately to make you miserable, she thought. "I've just been really busy. Especially with the contest."

"The Queen has no time for her most loyal subject. What's going on, Kiki? I've tried calling you the

101

past few nights, and your parents wouldn't even tell me where you were."

Oops. Kiki blushed. She probably looked as guilty as she felt. "Bobby . . ." She paused.

"Uh-huh," he said with a hurt-puppy expression. "I think I know what that means. Who is he?"

"Well, I don't have another boyfriend, if that's what you mean." Not exactly, anyway, she thought.

"Then where were you the last few evenings? And why didn't you return my calls?" he asked.

Kiki gulped. Now was the time. Here goes . . . "Well, actually, I've been in jail."

"What's that supposed to mean?"

"I mean, I've been visiting jail," she said. She could see that Bobby was getting more frustrated.

"In jail, visiting jail. Kiki, I doubt you've been playing Monopoly the past two nights. Next you'll tell me you passed Go and collected two hundred dollars." He shook his head. "I don't get it."

"I've been there because I've been visiting Spike." There. Finally. She said it.

"Huh?" A look of shock appeared on his face. "I still don't get it. What pleasure could you get out of visiting a murderer?"

"Bobby, he's not a murderer!" Her voice rose as she defended Spike.

"Look, the Queen's giving her prince the boot," someone yelled from down the hall. "A royal divorce."

102

They stared at each other for a moment. A long and painful moment.

"He's not the murderer, Bobby. I know it. It's not much fun being the Peach Blossom Queen when someone we've known all our lives is being unfairly persecuted."

"You really think that Spike didn't kill April? How can you be so sure?" Bobby asked tightly. "Did you look deep into his eyes and get some inside line on the truth?"

Kiki looked away. Bobby had summed up the situation perfectly. Always thinking so logically. Maybe it had something to do with him being the captain of the debating team, or maybe it was just too obvious. "Look, Bobby," she said, "we're talking about Spike Navarrone. Didn't you two ride bikes together when you were little? Spike, the guy who spent an entire day cruising all over Paradiso on his Harley looking for your younger sister's lost puppy?"

"Kiki, I know who we're talking about. We're talking about a guy who had all of us fooled. And apparently *still* has you fooled. Look, I feel really sad about it too. But we've got to face facts."

"Facts? You mean like Spike's confession? The fact is, he was forced into it. I know he's innocent, and I'm going to help him fight it."

Bobby swallowed hard. "So where does that leave me? Us? I guess I'm not as exciting as the criminal type."

103

"He's not a criminal, Bobby."

"But he *is* exciting. Right, Kiki?"

Kiki hesitated.

"Just say it. Let me hear it so I know we're finished."

No tears, Kiki promised herself. "Maybe it's for the best, Bobby. That way neither of us will be hurting."

"Fine," Bobby said, his face white, his tone icy. "If that's the way you want it. You know, Kiki, April was the first one fooled by Spike. At least in your case he's in jail, so he can't harm you."

Kiki's sorrow at having to break up with Bobby disappeared in a wave of disgust. "Bobby, it's not fair to condemn Spike just because he and I are—getting to be friends."

"Friends," Bobby echoed bitterly. "That's just great. It seems like I'm the one who's been condemned, not Spike."

Kiki didn't know what to say. "Look, Bobby. I didn't mean to hurt you. Really." There was a very uncomfortable silence. "I'd better go, Bobby. I'm really late for rehearsal."

"Pardon me if I don't bow," he said. He turned and walked away, slinging his backpack against his shoulder hard enough to dislocate it.

Kiki breathed a sigh of painful relief. As guilty as she felt, she knew it was for the best. That scene had been long coming. She reached into her locker to put her books away before rehearsal. There was something on the shelf next to her lunch bag—something hard and shiny. A wrench! Kiki gasped. *Don't faint,* she told herself. *Someone's only trying to scare you.* Attached to the wrench was a note: "You're next, Peggy Sue."

CHAPTER 14

"It's so great to be here!" Raven said, looking at all the familiar faces in SCAM.

"Welcome back!" Winston Purdy shouted.

"Long live the scrublands!" added Hope.

"Down with the mall!"

"Birds before big business!"

"Say it with flowers!" Eddie Hagenspitzel had to get the last word, as usual.

Raven could feel her cheeks flush with color. She was almost as red as the ruffled peasant blouse she wore with her favorite blue jeans. She hadn't felt this good since the day she and Vaughn had driven up to the Cutters' cabin. "Thanks, guys. Thank you for being here." She felt as if the real Raven Cruz had been locked up in Calvin Pinkerton's wall safe, a hostage of his money, and that now, with the money returned, she was free again.

But the hard part was still in front of her. She grew

serious. "I think before I reappoint myself chairperson, you should decide whether you want me or not."

"Of course we do," Winston piped up, adjusting the thick glasses that were forever slipping down his snub nose. Raven could see the tops of his brown socks below the too-short cuffs of his high-water pants. "If it weren't for you, there wouldn't be any SCAM."

Raven bit her lip. Winston might be a class A nerd, but he had a good heart. She hated to let him down. "Winston, wait. There's something you don't know." Raven could feel the nervousness coursing through her body. "I quit on you guys because . . ." She took a deep breath. As she did, the door to the classroom squeaked open. Raven felt her nerves hit new heights as Vaughn strolled in. Perfect timing.

He slipped quietly to the back of the room, but Raven could feel all her attention following him. What was Vaughn doing here? She tried to focus on the people in the front row: Hope, Winston, Jess Gardner, and Mark Delsley, from the wrestling team. Even Bubba Dole was there. Psycho could never stay out of a good fight. At least this time he was on the right side.

"Raven, because why?" Hope prompted her. "Why did you quit on us before?"

Raven let her gaze travel to where Vaughn stood. He gave an almost imperceptible nod, as if encouraging her to go on.

"Because," she said, still looking at Vaughn, "I sold out. I made a deal with Calvin Pinkerton."

A shocked hush fell over the meeting.

"No way!" someone exclaimed from over in the corner.

Raven nodded. She felt ashamed of herself all over again, as if she were walking away from the Pinkerton Estates with the money in her pocket. "Yes," she admitted quietly, rocking back on the heels of her cowboy boots.

"Wow. Maybe we *do* have to think about who's going to be in charge of this group," Mark Delsley said.

Raven felt a spark of fight flare up in her—the kind of fight that had led her to form SCAM in the first place. "Mark, for whatever it's worth, I'd like to explain," she said. "I think I mentioned when I quit that my mother was sick?"

Heads nodded.

"Well, there was more to it than just that. See, my family couldn't afford to pay her medical bills," Raven explained. She let the ugly conclusion go unspoken. As she looked down at the floor, hushed murmurs spread through the room.

"And now what?" Mark Delsley demanded.

"I went and told Mr. Pinkerton I couldn't do what I'd told him I would do," Raven said. She was surprised at how good it felt to tell the whole truth. "So now you know. I guess you'll want to elect a new chairperson for SCAM." She spoke matter-of-factly. She felt no self-pity. If anything, she felt a rush of relief. The guilt that had been hanging over her was lifting off. She looked at Vaughn. When he smiled, she smiled back.

"We knew you were with us all along, Raven," Jess called out. Some of the others responded with applause.

"I'll kill Calvin Pinkerton," Bubba Dole blurted out. "That lousy creep."

"Maybe we'll just kill his plans for the mall," Raven said. "I mean, you guys will. Now that you know what I did . . ." She looked over at Mark Delsley.

Mark shrugged. "I guess under the circumstances . . ."

". . . we all would have done whatever we had to for someone we loved," Hope said loyally. "Raven, you can't quit and then rejoin and then step down again. You know how far we got without you? Exactly nowhere."

"Yeah," chimed in Winston Purdy. "We need you." He stood up, and Raven watched him dig around in his front pocket. "If it's your mother that's stopping you . . . here." He pulled a couple of dollar bills out of his pocket.

Suddenly all the kids were reaching for their wallets.

109

Raven felt an unexpected rush of tears. "You guys are the best. But I can't take your money."

"Think of it as a loan," Winston said.

Raven shook her head. "I can't . . ."

Hope got to her feet. "Raven, maybe you won't take money from us, but I have an idea."

Raven wiped her eyes with the back of her hand. Her silver bracelets jangled. "You do?"

Hope nodded. "Kiki's been talking a lot about the April Lovewell Memorial Foundation. She's at rehearsal," Hope added as Raven scanned the room for Kiki. "But if she was here, I know she'd tell you that the goal of her foundation is to help the people of Paradiso—people like your mother."

Raven hesitated. She could hear Papa's words in her head. "I have never taken charity in my life."

Vaughn spoke up from the back of the room. "Raven, it's not so different from a scholarship," he said. Raven thought about how much she'd wanted to win the Peach Blossom contest for just that reason. She knew what Vaughn was trying to tell her. If she could accept the scholarship money for school, she could accept help from Kiki's new foundation for her mother.

Raven felt a surge of gratitude toward Vaughn. And toward Hope and Winston and all the other members of SCAM.

"So can I talk to Kiki about it?" Hope asked.

110

Raven gave a grateful nod. "Good. Then it's settled," Hope said.

"And you'll stay on as chairperson of SCAM?" Winston asked, leaning forward in his chair, all six of the Bic pens in his front pocket seeming to point at her.

"If you want me to."

A cheer of support rang through the classroom. "Hail to the chief!" Eddie Hagenspitzel yelled.

Even Mark Delsley nodded in support.

Raven was back on the job. "Listen, Senator Miller's only going to be able to stall that rezoning bill for so long," she said. "But if they bring the bulldozers in . . . we'll lie down in front of them! Yeah, that's it. We'll have a school-wide slumber party. We'll refuse to move!"

As the meeting ended and everyone was filing out of the room, Vaughn came over to her. "Hey, what you did today took real guts," he said. His smile held her, dazzled.

"Thanks," Raven replied. She looked into Vaughn's sky-blue eyes. "I'm surprised to see you here."

"Yeah, well, I guess you're not the only one who made a mistake," Vaughn admitted.

"But, Vaughn, what about your parents?" she asked.

Vaughn's smile vanished. He shrugged. "When I ran into you the other day, you made me realize that

111

I had to do what felt right to me. I'm staying at Jess's for a while."

Raven felt a wave of sympathy for Vaughn—and a funny, racing feeling inside as they stared into each other's eyes. "Wow, that must be really hard, Vaughn," she whispered.

He nodded. Their gaze was as intimate as a kiss. Vaughn touched her arm. She felt a tingle.

"Remember the first time I came to a meeting?" he asked.

Raven felt all the old emotions flooding back. She nodded. "I remember it was pouring out. And as soon as you came in, I couldn't keep my mind on the meeting. . . ."

"Neither could I."

"You asked me if I liked to dance," Raven said, savoring Vaughn's nearness.

"To see if you were going to say yes if I asked you to the Peach Blossom Ball," Vaughn said. He cupped her face. His hands were warm. "Do we still have a date?" he asked huskily.

Raven felt herself coming down to earth. She thought about how quickly everything had happened after Vaughn had asked her to the ball. Only a few weeks later, she was lying in front of the fire with him at the cabin—and thinking that she might be falling in love.

Then it had all exploded, just as quickly and furiously as Vaughn's temper. Raven remembered their fight outside the café—and the image of Vaughn with blood on his hands. If she gave in to her feelings for him now, would it end up the same way all over again? The memory of their fight was still so painful and fresh. Raven didn't want to feel that way again. Ever. She pulled away from him.

"Vaughn, I just can't rush into anything again," she said.

His chiseled features creased in hurt. He pressed his lips together and was silent.

"I—I'm glad you stuck up for what you believe in," she added. "Look, I'll see you around, okay?" Raven turned and rushed out of the classroom. She could feel Vaughn staring after her.

"Raven . . ." he called.

She kept going. If she looked back, she knew she'd be caught in Vaughn's gaze. Caught and trapped.

CHAPTER 15

Okay, just pull yourself together. You're the Queen, so act like one, Kiki reminded herself as she pushed open the door to the auditorium. She tried to put aside her thoughts of the threat in her locker and the breakup with Bobby. She took a deep breath and blew out all the remaining fear and guilt. There. Things would be better now. It was just a warped prank, she assured herself. Some trick of Lacey's fan club to get Kiki to step down. And as for Bobby, he would forgive and forget. She hoped they could even remain friends. Then the ugly thoughts crept back. I hope I'm still *around* to be his friend.

Rehearsal was already in progress as Kiki approached the stage from the empty, darkened seating area. Miss Crane was again directing the session using the metal folding chairs as stand-ins for the crowd. And in Kiki's place there was Lacey. She sat in a chair on top of a small wooden platform, waving down to her metal subjects.

Hate to ruin all the fun, Lacey, Kiki thought, but the real Queen has arrived. "Hello, everyone," she called out as she walked up the steps onto the stage.

"Quiet, please," Miss Crane said, waving a hand in Kiki's direction, keeping her eyes on Lacey. "Now, this is when the band will be playing 'Peggy Sue.' Did I ever tell you that's what the boys called me in high school?" she said with a schoolgirl giggle. "Your father, for one, Lacey." Miss Crane's first name was Peg. "You know that Pinkie—I mean Calvin—and I were good friends back then, don't you, Lacey?"

"You've told me that about a million times," Lacey said.

"We were very good friends," Miss Crane repeated, fiddling with the buttons on her baggy cardigan, a starry look in her eyes. "Your father and I were —very close."

"Excuse me, Miss Crane," Kiki interrupted, making a coughing sound as she stepped into her view. "It's me."

"Oh, Kiki dear. I didn't realize you were here. Well, come along now, we've got a lot to learn." Miss Crane took Lacey's hand. "Here you are, Lacey. Let me help you down."

"I'm sorry I'm late, Miss Crane. I promise it won't happen again," Kiki said.

"We were beginning to wonder whether you'd

make it," Miss Crane said. "Lacey mentioned that you might be having second thoughts, Kiki. I hope that's not true."

Kiki frowned at Lacey. Figures. You just won't stop trying, will you? "No, ma'am," Kiki assured Miss Crane. "I wouldn't miss this for the world. I love being Queen."

"Good. I'm glad to hear it. I'll repeat what I told you yesterday, dear. There is *nothing* like being the Peach Blossom Queen."

Kiki got a kick out of hearing Miss Crane go on about that "special" feeling. Rumor had it that Miss Crane had been the runner-up, way back when—to Lacey's mother! Hard to believe such a drab-looking old maid could ever have been a cute, bubbly beauty. But maybe that had something to do with why she was so involved in the Festival every year.

"Now, we're going to spend a little time rehearsing for the parade. This," she said, pointing to the wooden platform, "is our float. I expected the real one to be ready today, but now they tell me they need to fix a few things."

Kiki could hear the crew hammering and sawing backstage. The underclassmen were responsible for building the float every year. It was designed especially for the Festival theme. Kiki couldn't wait to see it.

"Miss Crane," Lacey said, "maybe I should go see if it's finished enough to use for the rehearsal."

116

Amazing! Kiki thought. She's actually being helpful.

Miss Crane liked the idea too. "Well, that way both of you could be in your proper places. Yes, that's an excellent idea, Lacey."

Lacey was up in an instant. "Anything to get me off the stage with you," she whispered to Kiki, shooting her a murderous look as she brushed past her on the way backstage.

"Now, I know it sounds simple," Miss Crane lectured, "but you are going to have to sit on top of the float, keeping your smile and maintaining your regal stature at all times. People will be applauding you from all directions, and it is important that you wave to each and every one of them all. No one wants to be slighted by the Queen."

How hard can it be to glide along on a float? Kiki ascended the makeshift float. She imagined everyone in Paradiso lined up along Old Town Road watching the parade. She gave her biggest, brightest smile while she waved to her cheering fans. "How's that, Miss Crane?" she asked.

"Marvelous, dear," she said. "Oh my, look!" Miss Crane pointed toward the back of the stage. Kiki twirled around to see Lacey pushing open the backstage curtain as the construction crew wheeled the float in.

"Wow!" Kiki was totally psyched. It was still unfinished, but it looked impressive, a massive wooden ve-

117

hicle, half ark and half car. In honor of the fifties' theme, the sides were painted to look like a vintage Chevrolet, shiny peach with sleekly sculpted fins in the back and a long hood that jutted out in front. The main platform had two gigantic bucket seats. The front seat had an oversized steering wheel. The other seat, toward the back of the float, was smaller and considerably lower to the ground. For wheels they had used huge black tires with whitewalls and polished chrome hubcaps. Kiki marveled at the hood ornament—a beautifully hand-carved, painted wooden Queen, with "Kiki De Santis" penciled in on the crown. But the Queen's hair was painted blond. Kiki made a mental note to make sure the mistake would be corrected before the float was finished. Otherwise it looked perfect.

"All this for me? Wow! Can I get in it?" Kiki asked, eagerly.

"Sure. You're going to love it, Kiki," Brian Campbell, Janice's younger brother, said. He placed a metal step stool by the side of the float. "Hop on."

Kiki got up on the float. "Wow, this is great! I'm going to cruise in this baby."

"That's your seat," Brian informed her, pointing toward the front. "It's not quite finished, but try it out anyway."

Kiki eagerly moved to the front of the float. But as she started to climb into the seat, it slid out from under her and the whole float rocked forward, practically tipping over. Like a surfer, Kiki shifted her weight and managed to remain standing, one hand clutching the steering wheel. She let out a nervous laugh. "Phew. That was some start, huh?" She wiped her brow. "Well, now I just have to learn to keep my smile throughout. Right, Miss Crane?"

"That's the spirit, dear," she said. "I assume you'll take care of that, Brian."

"Nice going, Brian," Lacey joked.

"Now, now, Lacey, there's no need for that," Miss Crane said. "Just the same, Brian, I assume you'll make a note to fix Kiki's seat. I expect everything to be working perfectly for the Festival."

"Yes, ma'am, of course."

"Well then, let's get on with the rehearsal, girls. Kiki dear, are you ready for some company up there? Lacey, why don't you take your place on the float?"

Kiki was glad to see that Lacey would be at the back of the float, as far away as possible, and not nearly as high up.

"What's this for?" Kiki asked, looking down on the floor at what appeared to be the gas pedal. "I don't have to drive this thing, do I?"

"It's for making confetti," Lacey announced.

"How do you know?" Kiki questioned.

"Uh . . . Brian told me," Lacey said. "Didn't you, Brian?"

Kiki noticed Lacey giving Brian a little wink. It figured that even though Lacey wasn't the Queen, she was still up on every little detail of the Peach Blossom Festival.

"A confetti maker, that's right," Brian said. "When you pump it, you'll be showered with the stuff."

"Cool. This'll be great." Pretending that a boisterous crowd was all around her, Kiki smiled and waved to everyone. She blew a big kiss and pressed her foot on the pedal, waiting for the colored paper to fill the air.

Brrrrrrr. Kiki was startled by a loud buzz. It was followed by a foul odor, and then billows of black smoke poured out from the floor. The stage was transformed into a huge cloud of thick smog. Kiki stood there, coughing, unable to see anything. The smoke kept coming out. The noise continued. "Help!" Kiki cried, as she felt a hand on her shoulder and another grabbing hold of her wrist and twisting it and bending it behind her back.

Kiki heard a garbled voice in her ear. "Are you gonna drop out or not?"

"Who's that?" Kiki shrieked. But everything was solid black. Whoever it was let go, leaving Kiki coughing and searching in the dark.

When the smoke finally started to dissipate, a big hazy mess remained. Kiki was covered from head to toe with black soot. Her bare arms were black as night. She felt ill. Kiki noticed Lacey was sitting in her seat, smiling, as if nothing ever happened.

120

All of a sudden it all made sense. So that's it! Lacey's got the whole crew working for her. She thinks she's going to intimidate me into giving her the crown. And that's why that hood ornament has blond hair.

A shiver raced through her. Kiki wondered what else Lacey had had rigged up for her. How many times was she going to test Kiki's determination? If she had paid Vaughn five hundred dollars to have her car fixed and had given April the Madonna tickets that everyone so coveted, what deal could she have made with Brian Campbell and company?

Kiki looked at Lacey, who was brushing the soot off her clothes ever so casually. She was wearing old jeans, a plain gray sweatshirt, and a baseball cap. Lacey would be in an outfit like that only if there was a very good reason—for instance, if she'd known exactly what was going to happen. She probably had another outfit in her bag to change into after rehearsal.

"Is everyone all right?" Miss Crane twittered anxiously. "My, my, you have certainly outdone yourselves this year."

"Sorry, Miss Crane," Brian muttered sheepishly. "I guess we have a few kinks to work out."

"I'm ready to continue, Miss Crane," Kiki said, glaring at Lacey. She was determined to go on, prepared now for anything and everything that Lacey had up her sleeve.

121

But Miss Crane shook her head. "Come on down from there, girls," she said. "I think we've done enough for one day. I don't know about you, but I could use a good shower. Let's hope that things will be functioning a little more smoothly tomorrow."

Kiki stepped down from her seat and went over to the side of the float where the step stool sat. She put her foot over the edge of the float, but hesitated when she realized that it wasn't the same stool that was there before. The one Brian had put there originally was metal. This one was wooden and bright blue. And it had almost no soot on it at all. Someone must have changed it when everything was in a cloud of smoke. Kiki could feel Lacey behind her, breathing down her neck.

"Well, go ahead," Lacey said.

Kiki backed up. "You first, Lacey."

"Huh?" Kiki noticed Lacey's shock.

"Go ahead, Lacey. I'll follow you down," Kiki said, looking Lacey straight in the eye.

"Brian," Lacey whined. He came over and steadied the step stool, holding on to it with all his strength while Lacey stepped down.

Kiki hopped off the side of the float. She matched Lacey's angelic smile as she walked by. "Nice try, but it's not gonna work," she said.

"Same time tomorrow, girls." Miss Crane was oblivious. "Bye-bye."

"Good-bye, Miss Crane," Lacey said, all sugary and innocent.

Kiki stared at Lacey in utter amazement.

"What are you giving me that look for?" Lacey asked nastily.

Kiki walked up to the stool, still standing there next to the float at center stage. She put her hand on it and pressed down. Instantly the stool collapsed in a pile. Kiki saw the embarrassment on Brian's face. And the fury and frustration on Lacey's.

Kiki's anger gave way to fear. If she had stepped onto that stool from the float, she could have fallen and broken her neck. Who knew how bad it might have been? She felt the sweat beading up on her forehead. She walked offstage in a daze. Lacey wanted that crown. Kiki was getting the idea that Lacey really was willing to kill for it.

CHAPTER 16

"At first I thought it was me," Kiki said. Hope watched Kiki dig her spoon into a towering mint-chocolate-chip hot-fudge sundae with mounds of fresh whipped cream. "Then I realized someone was doing things deliberately, to get me spooked. Then it got funky. Really dangerous."

"Lacey," Hope said. She sipped at her brown cow, pushing the vanilla ice cream around in the root beer with her straw. She liked it when the ice cream started to melt and the root beer got creamy.

Kiki nodded. "Lacey."

"It figures," Hope said. "You know, she's been one of my main suspects right from the beginning." She lowered her voice and looked around the Blue Belle Dairy, to make sure no one was listening to them.

"I've been keeping track of all the clues on my computer, and her name keeps coming up," Hope went on. "Who wears the same size shoe as the person who left a track outside school the night of the murder? Lacey. Who has a motive? Lacey. Who took tenth-grade computer science and would know how to leave me that message trying to scare me out of looking for clues? Lacey. And that hooded sweatshirt that Renée has? Lacey could have borrowed it, right?"

Kiki nodded. "Yeah, Lacey and I swap clothes sometimes. I mean we did. The Pinks do. You know what I'm saying."

"Yeah. Lacey could be the one," Hope said.

But Kiki hesitated. "What about her alibi? She says Penny was staying over the night of the murder."

Hope nodded. "Yeah, I know. But what if Penny was asleep? Or what if she's covering up for Lacey? You know how Penny would do anything for her."

"Like give her a wrench from her father's store," Kiki said.

"And rope," Hope added.

"Yeah, exactly," Kiki agreed. "You know, sometimes I used to think Penny was really jealous of me because Lacey and I were such good friends." She put her spoon down on the metal saucer under her sundae. "Best friends. It's so weird. I mean, until a few weeks ago, I would have been sitting here having ice cream with Lacey." She shook her head. "Don't get me wrong. It's been great getting to be friends with Raven, and now you, but I just can't understand what's happened to Lacey. I never would have exactly

125

described her as 'nice,' but she was really fun—a great person to hang out with."

"And you think she's changed?" Hope asked, mulling over all the clues that pointed to Lacey.

Kiki nodded. "Ever since—"

"The murder?" Hope prompted.

Kiki wrapped her arms around herself. "Yeah. I didn't even want to say it out loud. I guess somewhere, deep down, I was hoping the old Lacey would come back, and she and I would be friends again."

Hope felt herself tense up as she listened to Kiki. She felt afraid for her. If Lacey lacked niceness, Kiki had more than enough for the two of them. She clearly would have liked to find an excuse for Lacey, even though she herself might be the next victim. "Kiki, you've gotta look out for yourself," Hope said. "Don't forget that April had just been chosen Peggy Sue when she was killed." Hope felt frightened for herself, too. Jess had saved her the evening she'd been chased through the woods. But what if next time, he wasn't around?

Suddenly, the cheerful blue-and-yellow plastic booths of the Blue Belle Dairy and the clean, shiny counter surfaces seemed to be covering up the real nature of Paradiso. April had been stalked somewhere right here in town. By someone she might have known all her life.

"Hope, there's something I'm not telling you."

126

Kiki pushed her sundae away. "At first I figured it was a prank, but now I'm not so sure."

Hope listened wordlessly as Kiki told her about the wrench and the note in her locker. For a moment, she wondered if Kiki were desperate enough to concoct such a story to get Spike out of jail. But the fear she saw in Kiki's eyes was real.

"Lacey?" Hope asked.

Kiki shrugged. "Somebody's after Pretty Peggy Sue. Who would want the winner out of the way?" She watched her sundae melt into a murky pool of green and brown in the bottom of her saucer. "Tell me it's not true, Hope," she said, shaking her head. "I mean, looking back I guess I have to admit that I suspected the Pinkertons had something to do with it all along. But I thought it was one of Lacey's parents."

"Never Lacey?" Hope asked.

Kiki shook her head again. "I could buy the idea that Mr. or Mrs. Pinkerton did it. They always scared me. But Lacey was my friend for so long."

Hope reached across the table and gave Kiki's arm a squeeze. "I know she was. And I wish I could tell you that you're imagining things. But April's body was in my locker." The gruesome image of April's arm dangling out of her locker rose monstrously in Hope's mind. She pushed her ice-cream soda away. She couldn't take another sip. She tried to regain her

127

composure. "Kiki," she finally said, "the killer knew my locker combination."

"But, Hope, practically everyone at school did."

"Yeah, I know," Hope said. "But how many adults do you think knew it? How many people outside of school? Mr. and Mrs. Pinkerton? Seriously doubtful, Kiki."

Kiki blew out a long breath. "Someone knew my combination too. It keeps coming around to Lacey, doesn't it? Wow, it's just too weird. My ex–best friend might be planning my death." She shuddered noticeably. "Why? Why would she do it? Is being Queen really that important to her? Has it made her that crazy?"

"Kiki, think about what she did to you at rehearsal. Doesn't that tell you something about how much she wants to be Queen?" Hope asked.

"I know," Kiki said. "I guess I was hoping that maybe Lacey just wanted to scare me."

"Like she scared April?"

Kiki bit her lip. "Maybe that's all she meant to do. And it got out of control."

"It's possible," Hope said. "But it still means she killed my cousin."

Kiki's normally pale face went even paler. "I guess I have to face it. There was just so much pressure on her to win," she added. "She put it on herself. And her mother heaped on even more. Maybe she just cracked. I think I might if I had a mom like that."

"Whatever it is, we have to find out if we're right about Lacey," Hope said. "Before anything else happens." Hope felt as cold as the inside of one of the Blue Belle ice-cream freezers.

"And before Spike gets put away forever," Kiki said. As she pronounced his name, the fear on her face melted into a funny, dreamy look. Hope had seen the same expression in her own mirror the other day, when she'd been trying out a new way of putting up her hair—and wondering how Jess would like it.

"You really care about Spike, don't you?" Hope asked.

"Yeah." Kiki's cheeks turned pink.

"Well, we've got to figure out how to get him free. And get the real killer behind bars," Hope added. "In a hurry." Hope felt dizzy and sick at the thought of losing another friend. Maybe Kiki really would be better off giving in to Lacey and quitting the contest.

Quitting the contest . . . Suddenly, Hope felt a rush of excitement. "Oh, my God, Kiki. I just thought of something. A way to prove if Lacey really is the killer."

Kiki looked up, a sparkle in her eyes.

"Well, it's going to be dangerous," Hope warned her. "You'll have to go pay Lacey a visit. And you'll have to give up your crown."

Kiki was quiet for a few moments. "You know, at first I really didn't want to go ahead with the contest. I thought it wasn't right to choose a new Queen. And

129

I was scared, too. I felt like the whole contest had this curse on it. But then when I got elected, I started to really get into it. It's nice having a whole school and a whole town make such a big deal over you," Kiki said thoughtfully. "Especially after being Kiki De Santis, Lacey's friend, or Kiki De Santis, one of the Pinks, or Kiki De Santis, Dom De Santis's daughter. Now all of a sudden, I'm Kiki, Queen of Paradiso. It's like I woke up a rock star or something."

Hope couldn't help thinking about how all the fun and all the attention might have been April's. Her chest felt tight.

"But I'd give it up in a second to prove that Spike didn't do it," Kiki finished. "The Peach Blossom Festival means one weekend of glory for me—but it may be Spike's whole life. And April's memory." She banged her spoon down for emphasis. "Just tell me what you want me to do, Hope."

Hope began explaining her plan—carefully, thoroughly—as if her life and Kiki's depended on it.

CHAPTER 17

A cold chill ran up Kiki's spine. She stood on the front doorstep of the Pinkerton mansion in the somber gray dusk. She gulped. She had gotten this far. Now she had to go through with the plan that she and Hope had come up with at the Blue Belle Dairy.

She rang the buzzer and waited. Peering through a small, bevelled window set into the heavy, carved door, Kiki noticed that not a single light was on downstairs. A hundred rooms of darkness. She waited for a long while, ringing a second and a third time.

"Who's there?" Kiki recognized Lacey's voice over the intercom.

She paused. "Uh . . . It's me, Lacey. I need to talk to you. Can I come in?" A long pause. Kiki waited nervously. She felt as if she were at the front gates of Oz, waiting for the wizard to let her in and decide her fate. A deadly fate.

"I'm upstairs in my room. You know the way."
The door buzzed.

Kiki hesitated, then pushed the door open and let herself in. She walked through the marble entrance-way with its ominously-ticking grandfather clock, and up the stairs in the dark. Besides her heart, which pounded like a drum, the house was silent. It seemed that Lacey was the only one home. Kiki thought about turning back. How crazy is she? Kiki wondered. Crazy enough to kill me in her own bedroom? Her head kept telling her to run for her life, while her feet kept taking her up the stairs.

She knocked on the door and pushed it open. Half squinting and shielding her head with her hands, just in case, Kiki stepped inside the bedroom, feeling the plush blue carpet under her feet. Lacey was sitting at the chair in front of her vanity. Kiki met her wary stare in the mirror. Lacey was wearing a beautiful, pale blue silk robe and looked . . . well, face it, like a movie star.

"What could you possibly want from me? Need a favor from your humble servant?" Lacey snapped. "Forget it. Not on your life."

"Can I sit down? I have something important to talk to you about," Kiki said, motioning toward the blue swivel chair that she used to think of as hers—the best friend's chair.

"Go ahead," Lacey said sharply.

Kiki could feel Lacey's angry eyes following her in

132

the mirror. She sat down, remembering the softness of her favorite chair. Only this time it didn't feel the slightest bit welcoming. Everything in Lacey's bedroom was white and blue, so cold, the perfect den for the ultimate ice princess.

"Lacey," Kiki started, "I've been doing a lot of thinking about things. About you and me, and about the contest. If I had known that we'd be fighting so much, I never would have gone through with it. Certainly not after April was killed." Kiki tried to gauge Lacey's reaction as she spoke. But Lacey's icy expression was coming through loud and clear; Kiki hadn't struck a nerve yet. Lacey didn't flinch when Kiki mentioned April.

Kiki continued. "I know how angry and upset you've been lately. I guess it's all my fault. As your friend, your best friend, I should have realized how important winning the Peach Blossom contest was to you. Well, I want to apologize, Lacey. I never meant for things to get so out of hand. I'm sorry." Kiki saw Lacey's eyebrow rise.

"And?" she asked.

"And, I've decided to resign." Kiki saw the surprise in Lacey's expression. Shock replaced by immediate elation. She had finally won.

Lacey swiveled around in her chair. A smile lit up her face. "It's about time," Lacey said. Then a look of doubt came over her. "You really mean it?"

Kiki nodded. "Uh-huh. I thought our senior year

133

shouldn't end like this. I hated to see our lifelong friendship get destroyed. I'd rather see you being a happy Queen than an angry enemy."

"I knew you'd come around, Kiki."

"Well, I thought about the screen test, especially. It's key for you—it'll be your big break. I mean, I could never act to save my life." Although I just might win an Oscar for this performance, Kiki said to herself. Lacey was a pushover so far. She wanted to be Queen so much, she'd swallowed Kiki's act, hook, line, and sinker. Part one of the plan had worked like a dream. Now the hard part was just beginning.

"Friends, then?" Kiki asked.

"Best friends, babe," Lacey said, coming over and throwing her arms around Kiki. "You made my day." Lacey danced around her bedroom. "Now I have so much to do to get ready." She stopped in front of her vanity and looked at herself in the mirror. "What about my hair? Is it okay? I need a total makeover. Daddy will have to send me to Los Angeles to the best salon in the world. And—"

"You'll be gorgeous, Lacey. I'm sure," Kiki told her. "You'll be picture perfect. I knew I made the right decision. I'm glad you're going to forgive me for waiting so long."

"You're the greatest, babe. Really," Lacey said, still looking at herself in the mirror. "Hey, Kiki, about those little pranks I played on you at rehearsal yesterday—"

134

"Forget it, Lacey," Kiki interrupted. "I knew it was mostly a joke." Yeah, sure. Some joke. You almost killed me. As planned, Kiki thought, looking at Lacey and wondering how someone who was once so fun to be around could turn out to be so wicked.

"Hey, Kiki. You got plans for tonight? I'll take you to S.F. in the jet. We can go club-hopping. Like the good old days. Let's celebrate!"

"Sure, Lacey. That sounds like a blast." Kiki hoped that this was the right moment to initiate phase two of Hope's plan. She hadn't seen Lacey this happy since her first date with Jess. "Hey, Lacey, I've got a favor to ask you."

"Anything, babe. Shoot."

"Well, it's pretty serious, Lacey. You'd better sit down," Kiki said.

"What's so serious that it can't wait till after we celebrate?" she asked, doing a pirouette and dancing across the bedroom.

"It has to do with the murder. And Spike." Lacey stopped dancing as the words left Kiki's mouth. "You see, I'm pretty sure he didn't really do it."

"That's what I said from the start. But then he confessed, so of course he did it," Lacey said, looking puzzled.

"It seems like it. But I have a good reason to think that it didn't go that way," Kiki said. She studied Lacey's reaction carefully.

"You do?" Lacey was sounding a touch nervous.

Kiki nodded. "Yes, and I need your help to prove it.".

"If Spike's innocent, then who do you think did it?" Lacey asked.

"I'm not certain," Kiki said, her eyes fixed on Lacey for any sign of a breakdown. "That's why I'm asking you to help."

Lacey froze for a second. "But why me?" she asked defensively. "How am I going to help?"

Kiki could feel Lacey getting more and more panicked every second. "I want you to meet me behind school. By the tree with April and Spike's initials on it. Tomorrow night at eleven o'clock."

Lacey was turning pale. "The place where the murder happened? At the same time of night?"

"I wouldn't ask for your help if I didn't need it. Badly," Kiki emphasized.

"I don't know," Lacey hedged, "I'm just not sure, Kiki."

"Do you not want to go because you're hiding something?" I know you're scared because you're afraid the game's up, Kiki thought. Lacey was silent. "Are you?" Kiki persisted.

"No, I'm not. What do I have to hide?" There was another uncomfortable silence. Lacey's eyes darted around the room. "Okay, eleven o'clock. I'll be there."

"Promise?"

"I'll be there, Kiki," Lacey said, twisting a strand

136

of blond hair around her finger. "But I'm only doing it for you. Because of your friendship. If you'd give up the crown for me, then I'll do this for you."

Kiki breathed a sigh of relief. "I knew I could count on you, Lacey." What else could you do? Lacey would confess tomorrow night. Kiki felt certain now that Hope's plan was going to work perfectly.

"You can count on me, Kiki. But can't we talk about something a little more cheerful? Like being Queen?" Lacey asked. With the mere mention of the word, the smile returned to Lacey's face. "Oh, wow, I can't *wait* until Monday—then the whole school will know!"

How could she put her evil deed right out of her head like that and think about nothing but being Queen?

"When I show up for the ball next weekend, look out. Every guy in town is going to go wild when they see me in my gown. I gotta show it to you, Kiki. I just can't wait."

Kiki followed Lacey into her mammoth walk-in closet. Four racks of clothes lined one side. A storeful of beautiful merchandise. "After I lost the contest, I put the dress all the way down at the end. I just didn't want to face it," Lacey said as she pushed some jackets and dresses aside. "Here it is, the most beautiful dress in the—" Lacey froze. "April . . ." she whispered.

"What?" Kiki said. "What did you say, Lacey?"

Kiki could see that Lacey was trying to hide something from her. But Lacey whirled around and blocked Kiki's view. "What's the matter, Lacey?" she asked, trying to get a glimpse of what was there. "Come on, show me the gown."

"Uh, no. I mean, you can't see it. I mean—I—I just noticed that it has a stain on it. I couldn't show it to you like that." Lacey fumbled with a green blouse, clumsily dropping it on the floor, hanger and all.

The shoes! Kiki watched the green blouse drop to the ground, covering up a pair of large white sneakers. Lacey's mud-caked sneakers. That's what she was trying to hide. Not the dress—the shoes. The murderer's shoes!

Kiki started to back up toward the door. Just play it cool, she told herself. Play it cool and get out. Lacey all but pushed Kiki out of the closet and immediately shut the door, keeping her back up against it.

"What about San Francisco?" Lacey said, jittery. "Shouldn't we get going?"

"Uh, yeah." Kiki nodded. "I mean, no. I forgot, Lacey. I promised my parents I'd go with them to visit my aunt and uncle. You know, the ones in Sacramento." Kiki looked at her watch. "Oh my God, I'm really late already."

"You sure you have to go?" Lacey asked.

"Another time, Lacey. My parents will kill me if I cancel." Kiki gulped. Why did I say that word? she thought. "I'd better split. I'll see you tomorrow night at the tree, right?"

"I'll be there."

Kiki backed up to the door and opened it, her hand twisting the knob around without her looking. She kept a close eye on Lacey, preparing herself for any crazy move she might make. She gave Lacey a weak wave.

"See you," Lacey said, a forced smile on her face.

Kiki closed the door behind her and hurried down the stairs and out of the house. She was certain now. The shoes were the final proof. Kiki felt a painful sadness knowing that Lacey could actually have committed murder.

Then her sadness turned to fear. Hope was right. But were they in over their heads? Kiki raced through the darkness toward the gate of the Pinkerton estate. She was running for her life.

But getting down to the truth, the real truth, was going to free Spike.

CHAPTER 18

The Calvin Pinkerton room of Town Hall was packed. Raven didn't like being anyplace that bore Mr. Pinkerton's name. Still, it was hard to feel upset when so many people had turned out for the auction of April's art.

The walls were hung with her delicate, loosely worked sketches and watercolors, and her bolder, more vivid oil paintings, including a whole series of the scrublands at different times of day. Raven noted the irony of having them displayed in the Pinkerton room. But the biggest crowd had gathered in front of these paintings, and Raven heard plenty of oohing and ahing as people made notes in the program that listed each work in the order in which it would be auctioned off.

Raven felt an ache as she looked at the crowd. If only April had lived to see her own exhibit. Raven knew her sentiments were being shared. There were plenty of moist eyes in the room. She hadn't seen this many of the townspeople in one place since April's funeral.

But only a first glance said that April had brought them together. Anger and bad feelings divided the room. Nearby, the Reverend and Mrs. Lovewell were surrounded by a circle of friends offering comfort and support. Raven could hear Winston Purdy's mother saying how lovely April's drawings were. On the other side of the room, Mrs. Hubbard, Hope's mom, looked closely at one of the scrublands paintings— and studiously avoided the glares the Reverend was sending her way.

Lars Cutter stood talking to Calvin Pinkerton, whom Raven had been carefully avoiding all day. Darla Pinkerton, in black from head to toe, surveyed the crowd through her dark glasses. Vaughn was as far away from them as he could get. He kept his back to his father as he talked to Jess and Hope.

Raven studied Vaughn from across the room. He looked extra handsome in his blue blazer, faded jeans, and cowboy boots. Turning slightly, he caught her looking at him. The room full of people seemed to slip away. Raven tried out her best smile. Vaughn responded with one of his own. But as she took several steps in his direction, he turned away abruptly. She felt her heart sink. Maybe she should have told him yes after the SCAM meeting. Yes, Vaughn Cutter, I'd love to go to the Peach Blossom Ball with you.

Or anywhere else. Instead, she'd been afraid of how strong her feelings really were. It was her own fault.

At least on the small stage that had been set up at the front of the room, Raven sensed a little oasis of happiness. Mr. Woolery mimed banging down his auctioneer's gavel, pretending to bring it down on his hand. Kiki's laughter rang out over the room, like a silvery, fresh, cleansing rain. It hadn't been very long ago that Mr. Woolery had been a suspect in April's murder. Now he was smiling again—Paradiso High's one and only heartthrob teacher.

Raven noticed that most of the members of SCAM were here too, except for a few kids who had weekend jobs. Eddie Hagenspitzel was working the room—probably trying to get someone to listen to his jokes. Winston Purdy was taking a close, hard look at one of the scrublands paintings. Raven was surprised to see her little brother Pedro standing with him. Pedro's friend, Preston Powell, Paradiso's pint-size expert on birds and bugs and anything creepy-crawly, was there too.

Raven made her way over to them. "Hi, guys." She gave Pedro a light punch on the arm. "What's doing?"

"Raven, look at this," Winston said excitedly. A mechanical pencil was parked behind one large ear, as if he was just waiting for a math problem that needed to be solved.

They were clustered around a painting that was

142

rather different from most of the others. The colors were muted and somber, with only the barest trace of light on the scrublands grasses. The plants and trees seemed to be hiding shadowy shapes. Yes, there was definitely something in one of the tree branches. Raven peered more closely. An owl. Its disklike eyes were set above a hooked beak that looked like a weapon. Its razor-sharp talons dug into the branch.

"I wouldn't like to meet him in a dark tree," Raven quipped. She looked at the title of the painting, printed on a card next to it on the wall. "Night Bird," April had called it.

"It's true, he's a bird of prey," Preston Powell said seriously.

Winston peered at it through his Coke-bottle lenses, then cried, "He could save the scrublands for us!"

"What?" Raven stared back at the wide-eyed owl.

"Yeah, Preston's been telling me that this is no ordinary owl," Winston said.

Preston nodded. "It's a Speckled Nightflier. See the light-colored markings on its chest, and on the disk around his eyes? And notice the particularly short, sharp feathers on its legs."

"Preston, what does it mean?" Raven asked with a touch of impatience. She wondered if Preston lectured Pedro like this when they were digging up worms behind the café.

"Preston's trying to say that it's a very rare kind of bird," Pedro explained.

"Exactly what we've been looking for," Winston added.

Raven felt her pulse take off. A rare owl lived in the scrublands! Just what they needed to stop the bulldozers! Raven wondered how many weeks of waitressing tips she'd need to buy the painting.

The sound of Mr. Woolery's gavel rang across the room. "Ladies and gentlemen, I think we're ready to begin," he announced.

Raven took one more look at "Night Bird," and crossed her fingers. Up onstage, Kiki was taking the microphone from Mr. Woolery. She cleared her throat.

"Hi, everybody," she said rather shyly. "Thank you all for coming today. As you know, this is the first event to benefit the April Lovewell Memorial Foundation. All the money we raise will be used for community support. The foundation will benefit the people of Paradiso." Kiki's words gathered strength as she spoke. There was polite applause.

"I think it's only fitting that the first event for the foundation that bears April's name lets us all share the beauty she saw in the world," Kiki went on. "I'd like to offer a special welcome to April's parents, the Reverend and Mrs. Lovewell."

April's father nodded gravely. Her mother stood rod straight, looking right ahead, only the glistening

144

tears in the corners of her eyes betraying her emotions.

"And most of you also know Mr. Mark Woolery," Kiki said, "Paradiso High's favorite art teacher—our only art teacher, in fact."

Mr. Woolery raised his gavel in a wave and took the microphone from Kiki. "I'd also like to extend a special welcome to Reverend and Mrs. Lovewell. Your daughter's talent has touched me, as I know it's touched everyone here." Mr. Woolery paused for a moment.

Raven closed her eyes and pictured April, the sun in her strawberry hair as she sat outside school, sketching under a tree.

"I expect you've all had a chance to look at the art we'll be auctioning off today," Mr. Woolery went on. "It's very special to me, and I feel honored that I had a chance to watch April work and improve, and share her vision with me. I'd like to begin by offering the series of pencil drawings from her sketchbook, of some of her friends and people she knew."

There was a rustle of paper as the audience consulted their programs. Raven had studied the sketches when she'd arrived. There were two of Hope, one of Mr. Woolery, another of the Pinks, one just of Lacey, and several more of various different people. Spike was conspicuously absent. Raven wondered if Mr. Woolery had purposely left those drawings out of the auction.

Mr. Woolery opened the bidding for the sketch of the Pinks. Renée Henderson, standing over by the door with Doug Mattinsky and Lacey, looked happily embarrassed as Doug outbid Principal Appleby and bought the sketch for her for twenty dollars.

The picture of Lacey went to Calvin Pinkerton. But Lacey just stood there with this weird expression on her face. She probably can't decide whether to rejoice about Kiki giving her the crown or to split town, Raven thought. Raven hadn't heard anything, so she figured Lacey hadn't told anyone yet about being Queen. She probably wants to make a big show of it. Well, the only parade Lacey will be marching in is around a cell block, Raven thought, with a glimmer of satisfaction.

Next to Raven, Winston Purdy had pulled a pocket calculator out of his shirt pocket and was tallying up the dollars raised. "Three hundred ninety-eight dollars and counting," he whispered to her.

It wasn't bad, but Raven couldn't help thinking that just the lab tests the doctor had recommended for Mama came to more than that. The total increased as Mr. Woolery moved on to April's watercolors, and then to her oils, but the audience was responding more with a show of support than with large sums of money. On the other hand, the prices were low enough for Raven to bid with confidence when "Night Bird" was put on the block.

The biggest bid of the evening came as Leanne

146

Hubbard raised her hand in the air and called out "Two hundred dollars," to buy a bittersweet portrait of Hope and April. Raven applauded Mrs. Hubbard. It was as if Hope's mother had finally decided to acknowledge the closeness Hope and April had shared. Despite the family feud.

But April's parents didn't so much as turn around to look at Mrs. Hubbard. Willa Flicker, who stood in the back of the room, wrote fast and furiously. She always had an angle.

"And now I'd like to end by offering you what I feel are the most special works April ever painted," Mr. Woolery was saying. "The scrublands was an important place for April—as it is for me."

A cheer went up. "SCAM lives!" Eddie Hagenspitzel yelled. Raven grinned. Sometimes Eddie's big mouth wasn't such a bad thing. She noticed that Calvin Pinkerton was scowling and whispering something to Lars Cutter.

"The first painting in this series is the one titled 'Night Bird,'" Mr. Woolery said. The owl! Raven felt her adrenaline pumping. The bird that could save the scrublands! "The bidding will start at—"

"One hundred dollars!" Raven called out, raising her hand in the air. That was two weeks' worth of tips, but it was worth it.

Mr. Woolery looked surprised. "A hundred dollars? Very well, Raven Cruz bids one hundred. Do I hear—"

"Two hundred!" a deep voice called out. Raven whirled around toward the voice. Lars Cutter! Why would he want a painting of the scrublands? Suspicion took hold of her as she tried to calculate how many double shifts it would take to top Mr. Cutter's bid. Could she really afford to do it?

"Two twenty-five," Winston Purdy spoke up. Raven shot Winston a look of grateful amazement. "Winston . . ." she whispered.

"Tutoring," Winston whispered back. "I've been saving my money for a new computer program, but it can wait."

Raven stopped just short of hugging Winston. Her relief was short-lived.

"Five hundred," Lars Cutter said. A collective gasp went up from the crowd at the huge jump.

He must know something, Raven thought, dread taking hold of her. In her mind's eye, she saw the trees in the scrublands being torn from the ground by huge bulldozers.

"Five hundred twenty-five," Winston said. Raven couldn't believe the heights of Winston's dedication to SCAM. But ultimately there was no way he could outbid Lars Cutter.

"Five-fifty."

Raven knew it was a lost cause. Tears of frustration and anger burned her throat. Suddenly Vaughn was coming up next to her. "Raven, what's going on?" he whispered.

148

"That owl in the painting could be the key to saving the scrublands," Raven explained with hurried urgency. "I think your father's trying to buy it and destroy the evidence."

"Six hundred!" Vaughn immediately called out.

Murmurs spread throughout the room like a brush fire. "It's father against son," said someone nearby. Willa Flicker's writing hand was moving at supersonic speed.

"A thousand!" Lars Cutter countered. Raven felt herself gasp.

"One thousand five hundred!" Vaughn responded. "Granddad's bonds are going to be put to good use," he said to Raven.

"Two thousand dollars," Lars Cutter said.

"Three thousand," Vaughn countered.

"Five thousand."

There was a moment's pause. "Five thousand five hundred," Vaughn said, but his voice was growing tight and tense. "The bonds from my granddad aren't worth much more than that," he whispered to Raven. "If he keeps going . . ."

"Six thousand dollars," Lars Cutter thundered.

Vaughn looked at Raven and shook his head. His jaw was tight and his eyes glistened with fury. Raven felt her desperation spiraling. And then Winston was tugging at her sleeve. "Look, if we pool our resources . . ." He began punching numbers on his pocket calculator. "That's fifty-five hundred from

Vaughn, five twenty-five from me, and a hundred from you . . ."

"Six thousand one hundred twenty-five dollars!" Raven yelled, reading the total on Winston's calculator. She held her breath.

"Ten thousand," Lars Cutter said confidently. "And I'm prepared to go higher."

Vaughn looked as if he was about to smash something. "Damn it!" he yelled, for the whole town to hear.

An astonished silence fell over the room.

Up onstage, Mr. Woolery raised an eyebrow. "Did I hear another bid?" he asked mildly. But there was no other offer. "Ten thousand dollars going once." He paused. "Going twice." He paused again. Raven felt all her hopes dying. "Sold!"

"He won't get away with this," Vaughn said. He clenched and unclenched his fists.

Raven put her hand on Vaughn's arm. "Vaughn, calm down," she said. But he barely heard her.

Calvin Pinkerton was shaking Mr. Cutter's hand.

"He'll never get that painting home," Vaughn swore.

Around them, the stunned silence had given way to a loud buzz of voices. Mr. Woolery banged his gavel. "Excuse me! May I have your attention! The April Lovewell Foundation still has several more paintings to offer for sale." He managed to quiet everybody down.

Raven was in a daze. As Mr. Woolery auctioned off the remaining paintings of the scrublands, she bid a silent good-bye to the tall grasses and fragrant breezes, the bird songs and quiet walks in nature. But behind her bitter feeling of defeat was an altogether different emotion. Relief. With Lars Cutter's ten thousand dollars, Mama was assured of all the medical attention she needed.

Raven's emotions played tug-of-war with her. Unless she could track down that rare owl herself—which seemed unlikely without the sophisticated equipment that ornithologists use—the scrublands were gone. Her mother was saved. It was as if she was right back where she'd been when Calvin Pinkerton's money was hidden away in her closet.

The moment the last painting was sold, Vaughn stormed toward his father, his strides fierce and angry. "Vaughn! What are you going to do?" Raven asked, trailing behind him.

Lars Cutter was coming across the room from the other direction. A victorious smile stretched across his face. Willa Flicker approached from a third direction. They all met near the wall where April's "Night Bird" was hanging.

"Lars Cutter! That's quite a sum of money you paid for the work of an artist with no name," Willa Flicker said. "Would you care to comment?"

Lars Cutter gave Willa Flicker a hard stare. "May I remind you that this auction was to benefit the

April Lovewell Memorial Foundation?" he asked. "That's enough of a name for me."

It sounded good, Raven thought. But she knew the real reason Lars Cutter had made such an expensive purchase. "Mr. Cutter, don't you think you should be honest and admit that you have no intention of hanging April's painting?" Raven challenged.

Mr. Cutter turned his stare on her. "That's true. I don't," he said. Raven was taken aback at his unabashed nerve. "But it is a beautiful painting. It touched me deeply."

Yeah, as deep as your wallet and your plans for the mall, Raven thought.

"I'd like to come and look at it sometime, if you'll let me," Mr. Cutter said.

"Excuse me?" Raven didn't think she had heard right.

"What does Miss Cruz have to do with it?" Willa Flicker inquired, pencil poised.

"I intend to make the painting a gift to her," Lars Cutter said.

Raven couldn't find any words. She stared open-mouthed at Mr. Cutter. But Calvin Pinkerton, joining the group that was gathering around them, had something to say. "Lars, have you taken leave of your senses?" he thundered.

"If this is some sort of game . . ." Vaughn warned.

But Lars Cutter was shaking his head. "Son, I

don't think I truly appreciated what we would be losing until I saw your friend April's paintings . . . especially this one." He turned to Raven. "I thought you and your group SCAM were, at best, naive idealists in the face of progress and, at worst, troublemakers, rabble-rousers, trying to buck authority." He looked up at "Night Bird."

"But when I saw this painting, it reminded me of the nighttime walks I used to take in the woods of New Hampshire when I was a boy. And then I looked more closely. Well, my father, Vaughn's granddaddy, was a real nature lover. He taught me everything about plants and animals." Mr. Cutter got a faraway look in his eyes, his thoughts crossing a whole continent and several decades.

"So you see, I know something about birds. And I think this Night Bird is a lot harder to find than a new site for our mall."

"My God, Lars!" Calvin Pinkerton blurted out.

"Calvin, do something!" Darla Pinkerton demanded icily.

"You mean you're on our side?" Raven asked, happily amazed. She wondered if she should pinch herself to see if she was dreaming.

Mr. Cutter shook his head. "My dear, I don't imagine you'll ever be happy with our plans for a mall. Wherever we build it, trees will be cut down for the sake of business. But I think we might be able to find someplace less controversial to do our building."

"But if you wanted what we wanted, why did you bid against us?" Vaughn asked.

Mr. Cutter clasped Vaughn's shoulder. "I believe Kiki said something about this auction benefiting our community. Well, I learned this young lady's mother was pretty sick. And they tell me that the school needs a new music room," Mr. Cutter said.

Raven felt herself choking up. Lars Cutter threw aside his New England properness and put an arm around Vaughn's shoulders. "Son, your mother and I miss you. She said she couldn't bear to come today and stand in a room with us not speaking. Please, Vaughn, come home."

Raven looked from father to son. Vaughn's face was red, but he was grinning from ear to ear. He let go of his father and turned his smile on Raven. She melted into his arms.

"I don't think we'll need to have that slumber party in front of the bulldozers anymore," she whispered to him.

"No, but maybe we can have our own party in the scrublands to celebrate. Just the two of us," Vaughn murmured.

Around them, everyone in the Calvin Pinkerton room was talking enthusiastically—with the exception of the Pinkertons themselves. Raven watched them storm out of the room, marring the happy moment with a streak of darkness and anger.

CHAPTER 19

Lacey pushed open the door to Bolton's Hardware. "That's eleven ninety-nine for the tape measure, two dollars for the box of nails, and the set of screwdrivers is eighteen fifty. Will that be cash, sir?" she heard Penny say from behind the counter. Lacey felt her panic swell. A good half dozen shoppers formed a line at the checkout counter, just when she was desperate to talk to Penny.

Penny looked up as Lacey banged the door shut. "Hey, what's up, Lace?" she asked cheerfully.

"I gotta talk to you, Pen."

Penny glanced at the clock and then at the customers. "I'll be about fifteen minutes. Let me ring these people up, and then I'll get my dad to take over. He'll be back from lunch in a few. Cool?"

"Now, Pen!" Lacey said.

"Give it a break, lady," an angry guy on the back of the line yelled.

"Hey, that's the girl in the newspaper," someone else commented. "No wonder someone gave her a black eye."

Lacey ignored everyone. She looked at Penny with needy eyes. "Please." She was desperate. Penny seemed to understand her plea. She took a key from beneath the counter and locked up the cash register. "Register's closed. I'll be *right* back."

"Jeez, lady," someone on line huffed. "What about us?"

"I'll just be a minute. Can't you see my friend needs me?" Penny shouted back at them as she led Lacey past the angry line. "Let's go in the back where we can get a little privacy."

There was a little office set up in the stockroom. Boxes of screws and nails and loose tools were piled up high on Penny's father's desk. "Sorry it's such a mess, Lacey. It's always crazy around here." Penny sat down on the edge of the desk and motioned to her dad's chair for Lacey. "I thought you were going to the auction."

"I went. It was awful." Lacey told Penny all about Lars Cutter and the big breakthrough for SCAM. "And then my father started to go berserk."

"Well, I can see why. He's spent so much time and money on the mall project. He must have been ready to kill someone," Penny said.

Lacey was gripped by icy fear. "That's exactly the problem," she whispered.

156

"What do you mean, Lacey?" Penny asked, confused. "What's the problem?"

"Everything," Lacey blurted out. Her voice was shaky and she could feel the tears threatening to flow.

"Come on, Lacey, you're making me nervous," Penny said. "I've never seen you like this before. What's going on?"

Lacey looked at Penny through eyes blurry with unshed tears. She had to tell someone. She couldn't keep it bottled up inside her any longer. And Penny was her most loyal friend. "It's my mother, Pen," Lacey confessed. "It's *her*."

Penny's brow furrowed. "Lacey, what are you trying to say?"

Lacey crossed her fingers and prayed Penny would understand. "She's the murderer, Pen. My mother killed April." Her head dropped into her hands. She couldn't control her tears. She let it all pour out.

"Calm down, Lacey." Penny reached over and put her hand on Lacey's shoulder. "You gotta get ahold of yourself. Shhh. You're just not making sense. Everyone knows Spike killed her."

Lacey shook her head, her body still racked with sobs. "Everybody's wrong."

Penny pulled her hand back sharply. "What are you saying? Spike admitted it. You're talking crazy, Lacey. It sounds like you're the one who's going off the deep end, not your mom."

Lacey swallowed her tears and wiped her eyes with

157

the back of her hand. She told Penny about Kiki's visit and the muddy shoes and the whole terrifying conclusion she'd been forced to come to. Her mother had wanted her darling daughter to win the Peach Blossom Queen crown so badly, she'd murdered the competition! By the time she'd finished, Lacey's tears were out of control again. Even Penny looked scared.

"So you think Kiki saw the shoes?"

Lacey nodded. "I didn't even know they were there. But who else could it be besides Mom? She and I wear the same size shoe, but she wouldn't be caught dead in my sneakers . . ." Her voice trailed off miserably. "I tried to cover them up, but I could tell Kiki was freaked. I'm sure she thinks that *I'm* the killer."

"Did she say whether she went to the police?" Penny's voice was trembling now, too.

"I don't think so. But she's cooked up some weird plan at the murder site. Tonight at eleven. She said that she needs my help to prove who the murderer is. She's out to get me, Pen. I know it."

Penny hopped off the desk and began pacing. "It's a setup, Lacey. That part's too obvious. What are you going to do?"

"I don't know. I'm going crazy, Pen. What can I do? I told Kiki I'd be there. But I'm not gonna help turn in my own mother. I won't go."

"But if you don't go, she'll know you're hiding something. She'll stick her nose in even further.

She'll find out the truth." Penny's voice took on an hysterical edge. "What about the sneakers? You threw them away, didn't you?"

Lacey shook her head. "I was too afraid to even touch them." She started to cry again. "I just can't deal with this, Pen. I can't."

"Just be quiet, Lacey. Let me think." Penny continued to pace the tiny office. "Just let me think," she repeated. She picked up a yardstick from the desk and tapped it against her palm. "Let's see. First of all, you shouldn't go. No, you can't. You're just too nervous, Lacey. You couldn't handle whatever Kiki has in store for you. I'll bet she won't be alone, either. So you just can't know what to expect. No, you'll stay home. Safe and sound." She paused for a moment. Then something hit her. Her eyes lit up. Lacey knew Penny had the solution. "No, you'll stay home, and I'll go instead."

"You? But how will that help?"

"Just leave that to me," Penny said. "I'll make Kiki realize she's made a big mistake. I'll convince her, Lacey. Trust me. You do trust me, don't you?"

Lacey nodded. She was confused, but she believed in Penny. She had to. There was no other hope. "You really care about me this much? It might be dangerous for you, Pen. I don't know what Kiki's setting up."

"Don't worry, Lacey. I can take care of myself."

"Are you sure you can change her mind?"

"Just trust me, Lacey," Penny said, rapping the yardstick against her leg. "I'll handle her fine. By tomorrow morning, she won't mention a word about your parents. Ever again."

"I don't know what I'd do without you, Pen. You're really the most loyal friend in the whole world."

"What are best friends for, anyway?" Penny asked. "We are best friends, right?"

"Best ever," Lacey said, wiping her eyes. "Not like that fake stuff I told Kiki. She thinks she's so smart."

"Listen, Lacey. Why don't you go home and chill? Take a hot bath or something. I gotta deal with those customers. I'll call you tonight, after I get through with Kiki. Okay?" She took Lacey by the hand and led her out.

Penny's dad still hadn't returned, and the few customers that hadn't left the store already were still waiting in line. "It's about time," someone huffed.

"Jeez, it's like I got all day or something."

"Gimme a break, buddy," Penny snapped. She opened up the front door for Lacey. "Don't worry, Lacey. I'll fix everything."

Lacey walked to her car in a daze. She shivered, thinking about that night. While Lacey was sound asleep, with Penny on the fold-out bed right next to her, Darla was out murdering April. For a mall? So that Lacey would win the Peach Blossom contest and

make all her dreams come true? It was all too unbe-
lievable.

But Penny was going to help. Somehow she was
going to save the day.

CHAPTER 20

This was where it happened. The ponderosa pines loomed over the little clearing like many-armed monsters. The moon caught Hope, crouched on the needle-strewn ground, in a cold beam that slanted through the trees. She imagined her cousin's bone-chilling screams piercing the night.

But the voice that filled the hazy air was rich with happiness and excitement. "Imagine it, Hope. Me, a candidate for Peach Blossom Queen," April said in the soft, slightly throaty voice Hope remembered so well—a recording that sounded eerily like the real thing.

"Perfect, Kiki," Hope said. "It sounds as if it's coming right from the tree. But maybe you should turn the volume down just a little bit. You know, so it seems more ghostlike."

"Like this?" Kiki asked from behind Spike and April's tree.

"It doesn't seem possible," April's voice said, the words quieter, a whisper in the night. "Me and Lacey. Me and Lacey Pinkerton, candidates for Queen."

Hope shivered. She could feel her skin puckering into goose bumps. April's voice alone was enough to make her feel this way. Hearing it at the scene of her murder was infinitely more chilling.

She thought back to the day she'd recorded April's high-spirited words, as they hung out at the quarry after school. April, in a new green tank top that looked great with her green eyes and red hair, was snacking on a rice cake and worrying about taking off five pounds for the contest.

Hope was working on programming one of the school computers to "talk" to its users. "Just say whatever's in your head," she told April. "All I need is a sample of a voice. A few words."

"And the computer will imitate it?" April said.

"That's pretty much the idea," Hope replied. "You can feed in a certain sound by defining it with a mathematical code. If your math is right, it comes out sounding like the real thing."

"Oh," April said. "At least one of us understands that stuff." She shrugged. "Hope, do you think I look fat?"

"No, I do not think you look fat," Hope remembered saying with a touch of exasperation. "Now, how about if you talk about something else."

163

"Like the Peach Blossom Festival?" It had been the major thing on April's mind that afternoon.

Now the conversation from that sunny day was played against the starless night sky. "If I can even come in second to Lacey, it'll be a total dream come true," April was saying.

Hope wrapped her arms around herself. "Well, it sure scares *me* to hear it here." She went over to where Kiki was kneeling over a small cassette player.

Kiki hit the stop button, and then the rewind. "Me too," she said. Her voice was shaky. "And we know what's going on. When Lacey gets here and April's voice is coming out of the trees all by itself, she's going to flip. No two ways about it. Bet she breaks down and starts confessing right away."

"Well, I'll be right over there behind those bushes, ready to grab her if she makes a move for you," Raven said. Hope was glad to have Raven's support. She needed all the backup she could get. A picture of Lacey brandishing a large monkey wrench came into Hope's head. She stifled a cry. "Oh, April," she said softly.

Kiki stood up and gave Hope's hand a squeeze. "It must be awful for you," she said. "You two were so tight."

Hope swallowed hard and nodded. She put her hand on the trunk of April and Spike's tree, and found the spot where their initials were carved. A. L. she traced with her fingertips. *April. April, I miss you.*

164

Her fingers moved to Spike's initials. A. L. + S. N., with a heart around it, just like in the margins of Spike's books.

Hope's heart skipped a beat. *Wait a minute!* Spike's books didn't say S. N. at all. They said C. N. C for Carlos. And inside the covers of all his books, he'd written it that way, too. Carlos Navarrone. Every single time. C. N. Then why had he written S. N. here?

"Kiki," Hope said, her pulse speeding up, "when Spike writes his name, he uses Carlos. Even though no one calls him that."

"Uh huh," Kiki said. "His tools were marked that way, too."

"That's right!" Hope traced the initials on the tree once more. "But here it says S. N. Not C. N. Kiki, Spike and April didn't carve this heart into the tree!"

"Oh, my God, Hope! Are you thinking what I'm thinking . . ."

"It's a frame-up. Exactly!" Hope said. "And then they planted the wrench here so it would look like—"

"—Spike was the killer! Hope, you're a genius!" Kiki said. "Lacey sneaked out here and framed Spike!"

"Right." Hope felt like the giant jigsaw puzzle was nearly finished now. "I should have seen it sooner. Spike and April might never have been here. But Penny just happened to mention these initials—initials *Lacey* carved!" Hope thought for a moment.

"Maybe Penny was even the one who made them for her."

The snap of twigs in the undergrowth made Hope freeze. Oh, no! Had Lacey arrived earlier than planned? Hope shot Kiki a look of panic. "Hello?" she called out into the night. "Lacey?"

"What if I did carve those initials?" came a voice from the path that led to the pine grove clearing. But it wasn't Lacey's.

"Penny!" Hope whirled around. Penny's face was highlighted by the hazy moonlight. She had a wild look in her eyes. "Penny, what are you doing here?" Hope asked, her heart pounding a drumroll.

"Maybe I should be asking you the same thing," Penny replied. "You think you're so smart, setting a trap like this, don't you? Well, little Miss Junior Detective figured things out a little too late."

"Oh, my God. I was right about you, wasn't I?" Hope said. "You lied to me about this being Spike and April's spot."

"You helped frame Spike!" Kiki said, her voice rising angrily.

"Maybe I did," Penny said defiantly.

"But, Penny, you're protecting a murderer!" Hope said, her head spinning dizzily. "How could you know that and still do anything for her?"

"How could I? How could I? You just don't understand," Penny said. The moon flitted in and out of the cloud cover, throwing moving shadows on Penny's white, staring face. "Lacey is my best friend. Do you hear me? My very best friend. And no one is going to change that."

"Penny, you must be crazy," Kiki said.

"What did you say?" Penny's voice took on a menacing edge.

Hope felt a jolt of pure terror. Penny *was* crazy. Crazier than she or Kiki had realized.

In one swift and terrifying movement, Penny reached into her pocket and pulled out a pistol. It glinted in the moonlight as she aimed the barrel at Kiki. Kiki's eyes were wide with horror.

"Penny, my God! Put that thing away." Hope felt her heart pounding against her chest. She and Kiki were in way over their heads. "Please, Penny. You're frightening us."

Penny moved the gun barrel toward Hope. "I warned you not to snoop, Hope Hubbard. But you wouldn't listen. Now you know too much. I'm going to have to kill you."

CHAPTER 21

Lacey sat on the edge of her blue bedspread in her blue-walled bedroom and stared at her powder blue telephone. Blue, cold, dead—like April Lovewell.

Daddy, how could you? God, how? Lacey held her breath and hoped with every jangly nerve in her body that Penny was making everything all right, just as she had promised.

Come on, Pen, call. Lacey willed the phone to ring.

Downstairs, Daddy was drinking again, furious about Lars Cutter's betrayal. What if he went off the deep end—really off? Who would his next victim be? Lacey pressed her fingers to the faded bruises on the backs of her legs. Did she have to fear for her life? Daddy's own princess?

And Mother? Lacey knew Darla would stoop to just about anything to get what she wanted. But would she commit murder?

She clutched her stomach. *Please call, Pen.* What if something was going wrong? What could Lacey do about it? What kind of a trap had Kiki set?

Scattered images of the night April was killed played in Lacey's mind. Darla had practically passed out on the couch before nine o'clock. As usual, she was helplessly drunk. She had to be put to bed by the maid. Daddy, on the other hand, had been on his best behavior. He hadn't been drinking at all. He always put on a good show when there was company around. He had treated Lacey like his precious princess in front of Penny, her sleep-over guest.

But the mud-caked shoes that were still hidden away in the back of Lacey's closet were proof positive that April was murdered by someone in the Pinkerton household. With the maid and chauffeur off for the evening, and Lacey and Penny together all night, there was only one, dreadful conclusion. Which was backed up by the drunken argument Lacey had overheard between Mother and Daddy a few days after the murder.

"April Lovewell's death should have made Lacey a shoo-in for Peach Blossom Queen," Darla had raged.

"What difference does it make?" Calvin cried wearily. "The mall was the only thing that *really* mattered . . ."

And icy-cold Darla had hissed furiously: "That crown was everything! *Everything,* do you hear me?"

Mother, how could you do it, damn it! Lacey buried

169

her head in her hands. If only the phone would ring. Eleven forty-five and still no word from Penny—ever-loyal Penny.

Lacey remembered back to that fated night and how she and Penny had lain in bed with the lights out, talking about the Peach Blossom Festival.

"Of course you'll be Queen," Penny had said confidently. "It's guaranteed."

"Promise, Pen?" Lacey had asked as she started to doze off.

"You'll win. I know you will, Lacey," Penny had whispered.

Penny's comforting words had lulled Lacey right to sleep that night. She had even dreamed about being Queen. There she was on the front lawn of the town hall, the jeweled crown resting on her head as she waved to her fans and then . . . and then . . . and then, Lacey woke up. Her idyllic dream had been interrupted by the sound of the bedroom door closing.

"Shh. Sorry, Lacey. I didn't mean to wake you. Go back to sleep. Go back to sleep, Queen Lacey," Penny had said.

Lacey had opened one eye groggily, to the sleep-blurred sight of Penny taking off her shoes and sweatshirt, and crawling into bed.

Lacey gasped out loud. She hadn't thought anything of it then, but now, the murder flashing before her, Lacey saw it all too vividly. Who put their shoes and sweatshirt on over their nightgown just to go to the bathroom in the middle of the night?

And why had Penny kept trying to convince Lacey that Kiki was back-stabbing her? Did she think that getting rid of Lacey's other friends would make them closer?

Lacey suddenly remembered Penny talking about the Peach Blossom contest. "Face it Lace," Penny's words were coming back to haunt Lacey, "you're the only one worthy of being Queen. April Lovewell? Kiki De Santis? Raven Cruz? Give me a break!"

Lacey's teeth chattered and her body shook. Finally, she had hit on the truth. Penny! Loyal Penny Bolton! And she was meeting with Kiki right now. What was she planning to do? Kill her? Kill again to win Lacey's friendship?

Then you'll be the Queen, said the dark voice inside Lacey's head.

CHAPTER 22

Penny trained the pistol on Hope and Kiki. It gleamed eerily in the moonlight, silver and lethal. Hope felt her blood go cold. "That note on my computer," she said to Penny, her voice trembling, "it was you. And you were the one who chased me, too." The picture had become terrifyingly clear. "The one who threw the rock at me. Lacey didn't kill April, you did."

Next to her, Hope heard Kiki gasp.

"Hope Hubbard, girl brain," Penny said. "But you'll never get a chance to tell anyone what you know. No, Hope. It was pretty dumb for you to come here."

"Look who's talking," snapped Raven, her dark eyes flashing. "Just how do you plan on covering up *three* murders this time?"

"Penny, please!" Kiki begged, sobbing. She took a

172

step toward her. Penny waved the gun at Kiki. Then back at Hope. "Either of you take a step and I'll—"

"Put the gun down, Pen," another voice called out from the darkness.

"Lacey!" Penny exclaimed as Lacey stepped into the clearing. But she kept the gun carefully aimed at Hope. "I told you I'd take care of things. Why aren't you at home? Like you're supposed to be."

"Penny, it's too late," Lacey said. "I know what you did."

Hope had never in her wildest dreams expected to be so happy to see Lacey Pinkerton. Come on, Lacey, be a hero.

"Drop it, Pen," Lacey commanded.

Penny kept the pistol pointed at Hope. But Lacey continued to talk to her.

"Penny, calm down," Lacey said. "Come on, babe, cool it. I know how upset you've been lately." Lacey paused and took a small step forward. "We all know how horrible your baby sister's death must have—"

"That little brat!" Penny snapped.

Hope's shock and terror deepened.

"*I* was their child. I was the only one. Me. Penny Bolton. But it was never enough having an adopted daughter. No. They had to keep trying for their own baby. A real daughter. As if I wasn't one, wasn't real . . ."

"My God, Penny!" Hope blurted. "Did you kill your own sister?"

173

"Quiet!" Penny screamed, her voice cutting the air. She pulled back the hammer on the pistol. Startled, Hope stepped back, up against the ponderosa.

"She was no sister of mine. All she did was come along and turn me into the one nobody cared about, who nobody even thought about." She whirled toward Lacey. "And then you started doing the same thing. My best friend."

Hope stole a step toward Penny as she and Lacey faced off. But Penny spun around and jabbed the gun in Hope's face. "I'm warning you! Don't try anything! I have no problem using this. I'll kill you all!"

Hope stopped dead in her tracks. She pictured Penny, bringing the wrench down on April's head. Now Hope would be next. She looked toward Lacey for help. It was her and Raven and Kiki's only chance.

Lacey looked terrified, but she stretched a hand out toward Penny. "Pen, what are you saying? I never turned my back on you. I've always been here for you. Always."

"Right," Penny said bitterly, the hand with the gun shaking. "Like when you started getting all buddy-buddy with April? When she beat me out of a nomination for the Peach Blossom contest, and all of a sudden it was you and her? You got rid of Kiki with your scheming, but I had to get rid of April. For us, Lacey."

Lacey shook her head. "And so you waited until I

174

was asleep and snuck out and killed her. And you wore my sneakers—so you could blame the whole thing on me. I'm the one who's supposed to be in that jail cell. Not Spike. Is that it?"

"No," Penny said, her voice teetering on the brink of derangement. "I didn't mean to make it look like it was you. Taking your shoes was a mistake. I realized it the second I left the room and got a look at them. But I didn't want to go back in there again and chance waking you up." Penny gripped the gun, her finger twitching on the trigger. "I couldn't believe you didn't win. You deserved it so much, Lacey. But after Willa Flicker—she has such a big mouth—told me over the phone that April had won, I knew what I had to do. The whole thing worked perfectly. And after April was gone, I was the only one you had left. We were closer than ever. When I found out April was pregnant, and Spike had run away, it made everything easy. All I had to do was plant the evidence to show it was Spike."

Out of the corner of her eye, Hope saw Raven lunge at Penny. *Boom!* The sound of gunfire cracked the air. Hope screamed.

"Raven! Oh, my God! She's dead!"

"No!" Lacey shrieked.

"I'm okay." Raven's wavering voice came through the gun smoke. "She missed."

"The next one hits. I promise," Penny said, her words taking on a hysterical edge. "You don't think I

175

can let you leave here alive, do you? You too, Lacey. Why didn't you listen to me? I told you I'd take care of everything. Now I'm going to have to kill you, too."

"But, Penny, I'm your best friend, remember?" Lacey said. "Honest. All the attention I paid April— it was just a plan to make myself look good for the Peach Blossom committee."

Penny held on to the gun.

"I swear, Pen. May I get old and ugly if I'm not telling you the truth."

"Penny, it was always you," Kiki said, picking up what Lacey had started. "I knew I could never be Lacey's real best friend."

Penny lowered the gun a few inches. She looked at Lacey. "Really?"

"Put it down, Pen," Lacey coaxed. "They're right. I don't want to see you get into any more trouble. We all love you, Pen. Put the gun down, and we'll all pretend this never happened . . ." She took a tentative step toward Penny. Then another. "Give it to me, Penny."

But Penny shook her head. "No!" she screamed. "I know you're lying. Just like all the times you told me I was your best pal." Penny aimed the pistol directly at Lacey.

Hope was sure they were lost. She was crying now. "Penny, please. Listen to Lacey. Stop."

"Okay, drop it!" a man's voice called. Hope saw a

strong flashlight beam go on. She squinted into the light. As he turned the beam on himself, Hope saw that it was Sheriff Rodriguez, his own gun drawn.

Penny spun around wildly, waving her gun in the air, looking for a way out.

"Pen, it's over," Lacey said. "No one wants you to get hurt. Pen? It's me, Lacey, talking to you. Just put your arm down. Come on, babe. That's right. And let the sheriff take the gun . . ."

Sheriff Rodriguez went forward cautiously. Penny didn't resist as he disarmed her.

Hope went weak with relief. She threw her arms around Kiki, then Raven, and they sobbed freely.

"It's all right, girls," Sheriff Rodriguez said. "You're perfectly safe now."

Hope turned a teary-eyed face to him. "How did you know, Sheriff?"

"I didn't," the sheriff said sheepishly. "But I was having a slice at Mr. Pizza when I saw the Ferarri speed by. Lacey was going fast, even for her. I jumped in my car and tried to chase her. I found her car at the beginning of this path, with the driver's door wide open, as if she'd jumped out and run for her life. Then I heard the gunshot. I followed your voices, and heard enough to figure out that I have the wrong person in my jail cell."

Penny groaned and sank to her knees. The sheriff placed a hand on her arm. "Please, Lacey, don't let him take me away," she whimpered. "No, don't hurt me . . ."

"It's all right," Lacey said. "The sheriff's not going to hurt you, Penny. Trust me. Trust Lacey. You're going to get help. . . . Go with him, Penny."

Penny allowed the sheriff to help her to her feet. Hope dried her eyes on her sleeve and watched him lead Penny away. "We've all been through a lot," the sheriff said. "You girls go on home. It's too late for you to be out here. We'll take care of the paperwork tomorrow."

"Yes, Sheriff," Hope said.

Penny looked back over her shoulder. "Lacey . . ."

As the moon moved from behind a wispy cloud, Hope thought she saw a tear in the corner of Lacey's eye.

But then Lacey shook her head. "What a nut case," she muttered under her breath. "Boy, I'm glad I wasn't on her bad side."

Typical Lacey, Hope thought. Nothing rattles the Queen of Mean. But without her, Hope would have been gone. Dead.

CHAPTER 23

Raven sat cross-legged on the blanket, breathing in the sweet, fresh smell of the scrublands grasses. It was deliciously cloudy and breezy. The glaring, relentless sun that had been beating down on Paradiso almost nonstop since April's murder had decided to give the town a rest.

Vaughn pulled the cork from a frosty bottle of sparkling California white grape juice. With a loud *pop*, the juice bubbled up out of the neck of the bottle. Vaughn caught it in a crystal champagne glass. He poured the glass full and handed it to Raven. He took another glass out of the wicker picnic basket he'd brought, and poured himself one.

"To the scrublands!" he toasted. "And the girl who won over the big guys!" he added, quoting the article in the *Record*.

Raven held up her glass. Willa Flicker had put away her poison pen, for once, and the newspaper had given front-page coverage to the victory against the mall, touting Raven as Mother Nature's hero. She and Vaughn clinked glasses. Raven took a little sip, the bubbles tickling her nose.

"I have another thing to toast to," Raven said, holding her glass up again. "I've been saving it to tell you."

Vaughn held his glass toward her. "A surprise?" he asked. "Tell me!"

"To Stanford," Raven said excitedly.

Vaughn put down his glass. "You're going?" he asked. "But I thought you couldn't . . ."

Raven grinned. "Vaughn, this environmental group from Sacramento has been following the progress of SCAM. They offered to match the scholarship Stanford was offering me, and help me get a low-interest loan for the rest of the tuition!" She held her glass high in the air.

But Vaughn didn't pick his up. "So you've accepted?" he said quietly.

Raven felt her high spirits dissolving faster than the bubbles in her glass. "Of course I have. I wrote Stanford a letter yesterday. Vaughn, aren't you happy for me?"

Vaughn stretched his legs out on the blanket. "Sure I am, Raven. I know how much you wanted this." He paused. "It's just that thinking about next year kind of bums me out. I mean, you in Southern

California. Me all the way on the East Coast. We'll be so far away from each other."

Raven put her glass down and moved Vaughn's out of the way. She circled her arms around him and gave him a long, tight hug. "Vaughn, school's not even out yet. And we've got the whole summer together. Then . . . who knows? But today's so perfect." She traced the curves of Vaughn's muscular arms. "I don't want to miss a second of it thinking about what's ahead. Okay?"

Vaughn hugged her back, stroking the back of her neck softly and kissing the top of her head. "How'd you get so wise?" He laughed.

"Years of practice."

Vaughn ran his hands through her hair. "I missed you so much." His words were punctuated by tender little kisses all over her face.

"I missed you too," Raven said. "I kept thinking I heard your darned Jaguar outside my house."

"That's because you probably did," Vaughn admitted. "I drove by the café a bunch of times in the last few days, thinking I was going to try to make up. Then I'd chicken out and drive away."

"I never should have let you go in the first place," Raven said.

"Nah, you shouldn't have. You're right about that, too," Vaughn teased.

Their lips met in the softest, deepest, sweetest kiss. All thoughts of the horrible deaths she and Hope and

Kiki had come so close to disappeared. There was nothing but their kisses and the cool breeze and the song of the scrublands birds.

Somewhere nearby, the Speckled Nightflier slept.

CHAPTER 24

It was better than Kiki could have possibly imagined. Looking into the cloudless sky, she was sure the sun shone brighter than ever. High above the rest of the world, she sat regally in her bucket seat. She held on to the giant steering wheel of the sleek Peach Blossom Chevy float as it rolled down Old Town Road like a dream. There were hundreds of happy faces in the crowd. Kiki smiled and waved to every one of them.

She looked out at the crowd. She knew them all. Today, they were all one big happy family. Her royal family! She pressed her foot down on the floor pedal, sending a massive spray of confetti into the air, a multicolored snowstorm of joy. A boisterous cheer from the parade watchers followed Kiki everywhere.

"Over here, Kiki, over here!" Kiki waved to her uncle Bob. He'd been following the float the whole way with his video camera. Her little cousins, wearing

Peach Blossom T-shirts, trailed happily behind, stuffing themselves with cotton candy.

Kiki pointed to the back of the float so that her uncle would capture Lacey on film, too. Lacey gave a put-on, toothpaste smile. Kiki knew it would only have been genuine if Lacey had been up front, as the Queen, with Kiki in the back. At least Lacey was doing her best not to scowl. Kiki thought Lacey looked beautiful in her pink chiffon ball gown. It was the same dress Darla had worn years ago in the very same parade.

What a relief it was to be able to look at Lacey now without being terrified of what she'd do next! No anger or hatred. Kiki had even made up with Lacey. Really made up, this time. No ulterior motives. No back-stabbing secrets. Though she was pretty sure their friendship would never be like it once was, they had come to an understanding—they had made a deal. Lacey had promised Kiki that she'd be upbeat and graceful during the entire Festival. She'd be the sweetest, most dedicated lady-in-waiting Kiki could ask for. In exchange, when it came time for Kiki's Hollywood screen test, Kiki would ask Lacey to be her reading partner. Watching Lacey wave and curtsy like a princess, blowing flowery kisses as the float made its way toward the center of town, Kiki felt confident that Lacey would honor her part of the pact.

Kiki glanced behind her at the seemingly endless

184

line the parade had formed. The high-school band played right in back of her. They were as bad as ever, even though they had rehearsed "Peggy Sue" and other fifties classics for weeks. Maybe it was due to the fact that they had rehearsed sitting down in the music room. Somehow, the concept of marching and following the sheet music as it blew in the breeze, trying not to trip over the person in front of you, was a different story. Well, they're a little more in tune than usual, Kiki thought.

Directly behind the band marched the Paradiso High faculty. They were completely out of step, but it didn't really matter. Leading the group, dressed in an elaborate costume, was Mr. Appleby. He couldn't have looked funnier. Wearing a giant cardboard juke-box, he marched in super-awkward, jerky steps. The costume was exquisitely painted in a fifties style. "Peggy Sue" was the featured song on his costume, highlighted in shiny peach letters, as if to suggest that the music—well, noise—that the band was making was coming from him. The Dweeb was too much.

Dressed in a cheerleader's outfit from way back when was Miss Crane. She kept holding up the teachers' group, chasing after her baton, which was flying in every which direction. "Keep smiling, dear," Miss Crane called to Kiki throughout the parade. "Keep smiling."

Mr. Woolery, dressed in black jeans and a white T-shirt, his hair slicked back, was marching too. He looked every bit as cool as Buddy Holly and Elvis put together. A pair of giggling ninth-grade girls trailed after the handsome teacher. Kiki couldn't believe that just a short while ago she was afraid Mr. Woolery might be a murderer. She gave a wave in his direction. Thank you, Mr. Woolery. For being so understanding. And for helping this town appreciate April's artwork.

Kiki saw a huge SCAM banner a little farther back, waving in the wind. Two guys from the football team were carrying Raven on their shoulders all the way down Old Town Road. After each block, one of them would pass Raven off to the other.

The parade made its way to the town green, where a set of bleachers had been set up for some of the distinguished guests. They were shaded by a pair of oversized, painted Styrofoam peach trees. They looked more like palm trees.

Kiki waved to her parents, who were seated in the front row. Dom and Sue De Santis clapped loudly. They were wearing specially made matching T-shirts. Peach-colored, of course. Featuring a big picture of a queen with the words "That's our daughter" printed below it.

Kiki saw Sheriff Rodriguez, dressed in full regalia. He was beaming. She knew he was honored to be sitting next to her parents. The sheriff had written a formal letter to the governor of California requesting special commendations for Kiki and Hope and Raven

186

because of their help in solving the murder. He, too, had made Kiki feel extra special.

The mayor and State Senator Miller, who had worked hard with Raven on the anti-mall project, sat in the VIP section too. And Kiki saw the Reverend Ward Lovewell and his wife, Sara. Still shaken, their faces were tight. But at least they were there, fighting to go on with their lives now. Kiki thought about how hard it must have been for them to celebrate this, of all days. She said a silent prayer for April. She said one for the Lovewells, too.

"Man-o-man, here she comes. Pretty Peggy Sue!" T. J. the D. J., dressed in a wild turquoise-and-peach-colored sequined jacket, shouted into the microphone. He stood on a platform in front of the bleachers. As master of ceremonies for the parade, Kiki knew he was going to embarrass her a little with expressions about how "dreamy" and "neat-o" she looked.

As the float came to a stop, the marchers and the fans who had followed the parade crowded around the green to watch. "Ladies and gentlemen," T. J. said, "a warmest welcome to all. The Peach Blossom Festival is finally here! Right on, baby!"

A tremendous roar filled the air. The whole town stood together on the green. Finally, a happy event. Paradiso certainly deserved it. And this was just the beginning. The Carnival and the Ball awaited them.

Kiki remained in her seat, waiting for her cue to

step down and join T. J. and the others on the main platform. She remembered Miss Crane's words exactly: "This is where you'll tend to break out of character, dear. Everyone will want you to stop and visit with them."

Kiki noticed that Raven, having been let back down on the ground, wasn't able to keep her feet planted on solid ground for long. No sooner had she been deposited at the foot of the stage than she was scooped up by Vaughn, who was now enjoying a juicy embrace.

"Ladies and gentlemen," T. J. announced, "Lacey Pinkerton, the lady-in-waiting." Lacey began her exit from the float. Kiki could see that she was pouting.

"Remember the deal, Lacey," Kiki warned her through her smile. "Hollywood's calling. Don't forget the screen test."

Lacey immediately showed her pearly whites, and daintily curtsied to the front row of special guests, among them Calvin and Darla. Calvin was clapping. Darla, in her usual black, wearing her notorious dark sunglasses, refused to smile.

As Lacey finished her bow, she was handed a bouquet of roses by Junior Cutter. Kiki noticed a sudden sparkle in her eyes. She could tell that Lacey's smile was for real now. And she noticed that Junior's grin looked a touch more than innocent. Lacey, cool as ever, plucked a rose from the bunch and tossed it behind her, into the applauding crowd. Then she held out her hand for Junior to kiss.

Always on center stage, that girl, Kiki thought as she watched Lacey wink at Junior and then take her place on the platform.

"And now, for the moment you've all been waiting for," T. J.'s famous voice roared, "the one and only, Paradiso's favorite, the beautiful Peach Blossom Queen, Miss Kiki De Santis!"

A flurry of streamers shot through the air. Kiki, smiling but a little shaky, stepped down off the float. She had promised herself that she would make a bee-line for the main platform, even though everyone was calling out her name and reaching for her. But she noticed something that made her change her mind.

Standing off to the side of the bleachers, practically hidden in its shade, was Spike. His biker's attire —black leather jacket, jeans, and a white T-shirt— was no fifties getup. He was the real thing. Cool and smooth. So handsome. And free! Her dream of dreams had come true.

Kiki hopped off the float and ran toward Spike. She reached out for him to take her hand. He glanced around at all the people. He hesitated, then took her hand in his. On tiptoes, Kiki whispered into his ear. "Come join the party, Spike. You're free now."

Kiki led him out from the shadows into the gleam-

189

ing California sunlight. She looked deep into his eyes. In front of the whole town of Paradiso, their lips met. A warm, passionate embrace. She could feel all the electricity of the day in the touch of Spike's lips.

CHAPTER 25

"I may be the lady-in-waiting, but Junior thinks I'm the greatest," Lacey said as she applied a fresh coat of Peach Passion lip gloss. "I mean Lars. I don't think I'll ever get used to calling him that." She and Renée stood before the mirror in the girls' bathroom at school, fixing their makeup. Through the open window of the bathroom, Lacey could hear all the excited voices out on the back lawn, where the Festival was just getting under way.

"You looked great on the float, Lacey. Everyone was saying how beautiful you were. Junior, especially." Renée giggled.

"Smitten. Who's surprised? I guess I was just blessed with the right something," Lacey said, smiling at herself in the mirror.

"Hey, Lacey, have you been thinking about Penny as much as I have, the past few days?" Renée asked.

"Penny? What about her?"

191

"I don't know. I mean, I feel sorry for her."

Lacey caught Renée's eye in the mirror. She could tell that her friend was shaken pretty badly. "Give me a break. You feel sorry for her?"

"Well, yeah. I mean, she was one of our best friends. I thought about visiting her at the hospital, but I was afraid to go alone. It would have given me bad memories. I don't know—I thought maybe we could go together sometime. Just to see how she's doing."

"No way, babe. Not me. I always knew Penny had a screw loose." Lacey saw the hurt in Renée's eyes. "Sorry, babe, I forgot about your little spell." She put a sympathetic arm around Renée. "But you're all better now, Renée. And besides, that was different. Penny's big-time crazy. Capital C. You weren't a murderer, Renée. Penny killed April, remember. And her baby sister. It's better for both of us to stay away. Trust me, babe."

Renée nodded. "I guess you're right, Lacey."

There was a loud knock on the door. "You gonna make me wait all day?" All of a sudden Doug Mattinsky pushed open the door and came into the girls' bathroom. "Oops. Sorry, Lacey," he said, his face turning red. "Didn't know you were in here, too."

"Doug, get out!" Renée shouted, shooing him away with her hairbrush. "I'll be right there. Jeez."

"Boys." Lacey laughed. "Did you see the look on

192

his face when he saw me? It's like I was from another planet or something."

Renée ran the brush through her wild red mane. "How do I look, Lacey?"

"Gorgeous, of course. Like my good friend should."

"Thanks. Well, since Doug's so impatient . . ."

"Go for it, Renée. I'll see you soon," Lacey said, all but pushing Renée out. She locked the bathroom door behind her. Finally she could be alone for a minute. She could take off the silly peaches-and-cream expression that she'd been wearing all day.

Lacey went back to the mirror that hung over the bathroom sink. She turned the faucet on and rinsed her hands as she looked into the mirror. *Junior sees how beautiful I am. Why didn't the Peach Blossom committee?* She might have put on a great show for all of Paradiso, but none of this was fun at all.

Cheer up, babe, Lacey told herself as she tried to make herself smile. *Maybe things aren't as bad as you think.* Junior was crazy about her. He was super cute, sophisticated, and older. Lacey tingled, thinking about how all the high school boys couldn't hold a candle to her college fling.

And Daddy loves me, too. I'll always be his princess. She pulled up her gown and looked down at her legs. *Almost all healed.* Daddy hadn't taken his anger out on her since before the auction.

Best of all was her shot at Hollywood. *After every-*

thing she and Kiki had been through since the contest had begun, Kiki had turned out to be a true Pink in the end. Lacey would get her big chance. The talent scouts were going to see Lacey at her best. Madonna, Michelle Pfeiffer, Winona Ryder, look out. Lacey's coming to town.

Lacey heard the bathroom doorknob being turned from outside. "Just a second," she called. Then, an impatient series of knocks. "Hang on!"

But whoever it was continued trying to get in. "Junior, is that you? Patience, sweetie, I told you I'd meet you at the kissing booth. Be a doll and wait for me outside, would you?" Lacey asked.

There was no reply.

"Junior?"

Again, silence on the other end. "Lars?" Only the sound of the running faucet, the water swishing against the cool white porcelain sink, and the voices of the carnival-goers outside.

The doorknob rattled again. Lacey felt a shiver go through her. "Junior, it isn't funny. Is that you?"

In the mirror, Lacey fixed her gaze on the door. The knob began to twist, slowly and quietly. Just a slight squeak of metal could be heard over the sound of the rushing water.

"Who's there?" Lacey cried out. "Who is it? You're scaring me."

Lacey froze as she saw a thin plastic card being slipped through the edge of the door. Whoever it was

was trying to find the hook that kept the door locked. Her heart raced at a frantic pace. She looked around for something to use as a weapon. A broom, a plunger, anything. But Lacey found nothing.

She heard a distant laugh coming from outside on the back lawn. Lacey looked up at the small, open window. The plastic card searched for the latch. She had to hurry. Lacey jumped up onto the countertop next to the sink. The window was still a long reach. The door jiggled furiously. Lacey turned to see that the plastic card had located the lock.

Her adrenaline pumping, she jumped up and grabbed hold of the metal window frame. With all her strength, she struggled to pull herself through the window, managing to slip through the narrow opening. She could hear the door to the bathroom being pushed open just as she tumbled to the ground, barely feeling her fall onto the grass below.

Lacey got to her feet quickly and sprinted toward the crowd. She spotted Junior waiting at the booth. She threw herself into his arms.

"Well, it's about time, Lacey. Thought I might have to find another date. Not as pretty as you, of course."

Lacey was in tears. She shivered in his arms.

"Hey, you're crying, Lacey."

"S-s-someone's after me, Junior," Lacey sobbed.

"Huh?"

"Really." Lacey looked up at Junior, and saw the doubt in his eyes. "It's the truth, Junior."

"Hey, what happened to your dress, Lacey? It's ripped."

Lacey looked down to see a long tear in the skirt of her pink chiffon gown. She looked over at the open window, shaking with fright as she pointed to it. "He chased me out of there."

"Who, Lacey? Who chased you?"

"I don't know. I didn't see him. But you gotta believe me, Junior. There's someone after me."

Junior pulled Lacey close. "Shh," he said as he patted the top of her head. "Shh. Calm down, baby. I think it's been a long day, Lacey. In fact, it seems like it's been a long month. All the excitement and craziness around Paradiso has got you all mixed up. Shh," Junior whispered as he gently kissed her on the cheek. "It's going to be fine."

Lacey looked deep into Junior's blue-green eyes. She wanted to believe him, but she knew she hadn't imagined that scene in the bathroom. "Are you sure, Junior? No one's after me? No one's trying to hurt me?"

Junior shook his head. "No one. Promise, Lacey. I promise." He wiped the tears from Lacey's face. "Tell you what. How about if we go for a cruise in the BMW? This kids' stuff can wait."

Lacey nodded.

Junior put a strong arm around her shoulder. "We

could drive out to the quarry and go swimming. Just the two of us. With everybody here, we ought to have the whole place to ourselves. We'll be all alone."

"Great idea," Lacey said. She could already feel the cold, clear water of the quarry—and Junior's warm embrace as they dried off on the rocks. Yeah. The Peach Blossom Festival wasn't turning out so badly after all.

CHAPTER 26

Same as ever, Hope thought. Two scrambled eggs, three pancakes, six strips of bacon, well done. Her favorite breakfast. And for Mom, two slices of low-cal wheat toast cut diagonally and spread with butter. But Hope sat at the table and stared at the food on her plate. Her appetite hadn't woken up with the rest of her. Same as ever. Except that nothing is ever going to feel the same again.

"Morning, honey," Leanne Hubbard sang out as she came into the kitchen. She walked soundlessly across the room, her steps cushioned by her white, rubber-soled nurse's shoes, and planted a kiss on Hope's cheek.

"Morning, Mom. Your toast's on the counter."

"Thanks," Leanne said. She brought the toast to the table and sat down across from Hope. "All recovered from the big weekend?" she asked.

Hope shrugged. The peach-colored nail polish

she'd applied so carefully before the Ball was already beginning to chip.

"I know," Leanne Hubbard said sympathetically. "You spend so much time planning and thinking about the big event, and then it's over so quickly."

"Yeah," Hope said. But it was more than just the end of the Peach Blossom Festival. She squeezed a stream of honey over the mound on her plate. *Sacramento Valley Honey,* the label read. *Best Honey East of Eden.* She still didn't feel much like eating. She took a small bite of bacon and put her fork down. "Mom, how could she be going to school with us every day, and talking about the Peach Blossom Festival and acting like everything was totally normal? And no one had any idea!" Hope's voice rose as her anger spiraled inside her.

"Penny?" Leanne frowned. "Hope, I wish I could give you a good answer. But there's no way to make sense out of something so violent and brutal and pointless." Leanne reached across the table and took Hope's trembling hand in hers. "Honey, it's easy to feel this way about Penny, to have all your sadness and anger go into hating her. But it's not going to bring April back."

Hope closed her eyes and imagined April's round, freckled face, framed by a cloud of golden-red hair. In Hope's private picture, April was smiling. "I don't think April hated anybody," Hope said softly, opening her eyes and looking across the table at her mother. "I wonder what she would have said about Penny?"

Leanne sat quietly in her nurse's uniform and let Hope answer her own question.

"She probably would have felt sorry for her in some weird way," Hope said. "Because Penny is so crazy and mixed-up and feels so unloved." Hope tried to let go of her anger. Out of love for April. But it was too tightly bound to the tidal wave of pain she felt. She missed her cousin so much. "Mom, do you think I'm ever going to wake up in the morning not thinking about April?"

Hope wasn't sure whether she wanted that to happen or not. It was awful to start every day with a knot of hurt and anger and sadness. But if she stopped thinking about April, then her cousin would really, truly be gone.

"Honey, it's going to get easier," Leanne promised. "I'm not saying the pain is ever going to go away completely, but you'll be able to remember all the good times without getting so twisted up inside." Leanne gave her a warm, sad smile.

"I guess," Hope said. She managed a tiny smile back.

Outside, a song bird chirped. The early morning mist had burned off. Light streamed in the kitchen windows and bathed the room in California sunshine. It was the beginning of another beautiful day in Paradiso.

200

A selected list of titles available from Teens

While every effort is made to keep prices low, it is sometimes necessary to increase prices at short notice. Mandarin Paperbacks reserves the right to show new retail prices on covers which may differ from those previously advertised in the text or elsewhere.

The prices shown below were correct at the time of going to press.

☐	7497 0095 5	**Among Friends**	Caroline B Cooney	£2.99
☐	7497 0145 5	**Through the Nightsea Wall**	Otto Coontz	£2.99
☐	7497 0582 5	**The Promise**	Monica Hughes	£2.99
☐	7497 0171 4	**One Step Beyond**	Pete Johnson	£2.50
☐	7497 0281 8	**The Homeward Bounders**	Diana Wynne Jones	£2.99
☐	7497 0312 1	**The Changeover**	Margaret Mahy	£2.99
☐	7497 0473 X	**Shellshock**	Anthony Masters	£2.99
☐	7497 0323 7	**Silver**	Norma Fox Mazer	£3.50
☐	7497 0325 3	**The Girl of his Dreams**	Harry Mazer	£2.99
☐	7497 0280 X	**Beyond the Labyrinth**	Gillian Rubinstein	£2.50
☐	7497 0558 2	**Frankie's Story**	Catherine Sefton	£2.50
☐	7497 0009 2	**Secret Diary of Adrian Mole**	Sue Townsend	£2.99
☐	7497 0333 4	**Plague 99**	Jean Ure	£2.99
☐	7497 0147 1	**A Walk on the Wild Side**	Robert Westall	£2.99

All these books are available at your bookshop or newsagent, or can be ordered direct from the publisher. Just tick the titles you want and fill in the form below.

Mandarin Paperbacks, Cash Sales Department, PO Box 11, Falmouth, Cornwall TR10 9EN.

Please send cheque or postal order, no currency, for purchase price quoted and allow the following for postage and packing:

UK including BFPO	£1.00 for the first book, 50p for the second and 30p for each additional book ordered to a maximum charge of £3.00.
Overseas including Eire	£2 for the first book, £1.00 for the second and 50p for each additional book thereafter.

NAME (Block letters) ....

ADDRESS ....

....

☐ I enclose my remittance for ....

☐ I wish to pay by Access/Visa Card Number

Expiry Date